HILL COUNTRY

Gene Hill

HILL COUNTRY

Illustrated with drawings by Tom Hennessey

A Sunrise Book | *E.P. Dutton*

For information contact:
E. P. Dutton, 2 Park Avenue, New York, N.Y. 10016

Library of Congress Cataloging in Publication Data

Hill, Gene.
Hill country.

1. Hunting—Anecdotes, facetiae, satire, etc.
2. Fishing—Anecdotes, facetiae, satire, etc.
I. Title.
SK33.H656   799.2'02'07   78-6988

ISBN: 0-87690-297-2

Published simultaneously in Canada by
Clarke, Irwin & Company Limited, Toronto and Vancouver

Designed by The Etheredges

10 9 8 7 6 5 4 3

For Pop

CONTENTS

WELCOME TO HILL COUNTRY

Hill Country is neither here nor there. It's the place just over the next rise, that soft pool around the next bend of the stream, or the cover you always planned to hunt but somehow never did.

It's the hollow that owls call from in the dead of winter; the thicket that a whitetail always disappears into before you've gotten quite unwound. It's the circle where the big trout was rising before the little one took your fly. It's the cover that's full of birds but too thick to shoot, or where your best bird dog always chooses to exhibit his worst behavior.

Hill Country is littered with flies in trees, three empty shells and no feathers, lost dog whistles and forgotten pocketknives. It's the place where if you find enough old tobacco in the pocket of your hunting coat to fill your pipe, you don't have any dry matches, or, just as bad, vice versa.

It's the place where the best places to cast from are always two inches deeper than your waders can handle, where the sun is always in your eyes on the easy straightaway shots, and whoever you take there fishing or gunning always has his best day while you have one you'd rather forget—but nobody lets you.

One nice thing about it, though, is that the experts are rarely there. Hill Country is for the so-called *average*. Me, for instance. At least on a good day. I was once described as "looking like a badly tied fly." My follow-through on the skeet field has been likened to a blind man trying to hit a mouse with a broom handle. But it's a pleasant place for the idler, the man who pretends to be observing the feeding pattern of bass but who is secretly charmed by the minnow-chasing heron that has nearly all his attention.

Here we can take our dusking walks together, warmed by the thought that the evening star foretells a delightful tomorrow. Off in the meadow beyond the pond we can hear the roosting pheasants call for quiet and marvel that the thumb-size tree frogs can be so full of vocal spring. There's really a lot going on: the pleasant, inconsequential, forever fascinating web of things to do and see and simply listen to that weaves us into the pattern of our kind of out-of-doors.

This is no place to learn much. One of the things I do best is make a bourbon and water. Some say my wind knots set a new standard, and others have marveled at my ability to upset a dockside canoe. If there was an award for *low* when it came to choosing the Outdoorsman of the Year, I'd be well up there, or down there, however you see it.

Needless to say, none of this deters me a whit. I press on: in water over my boots; spoiling a hardheaded dog; dozing on deer stands; flaring ducks with my feeding call; and being somewhat confused about exactly where I left the car.

Hill Country is a place for people who relentlessly believe that the answer to their casting touch is a new fly rod; that the problems with right angles from Station 5 can be solved with another trap gun. They are convinced out of all touch with reality that the new parka won't leak like the last one, and that riding a horse is nearly a death-defying act. We are forever secretly surprised, but outwardly blasé, when we take a trout on a dry fly or a grouse on a sudden flush.

But none of this really matters. As long as there's still a thrill in finding a forgotten pipe in an old coat, having a dog that will frequently come when you whistle, remembering to bring your Thermos into the duck blind, and having a friend who thinks just the way you do, it's hard to have what we'd call a bad day.

We can also make Hill Country be anything we want. It can be a place where there is always a puppy to play with, where the notes from our duck call are celestially clear and irresistible to the skittery red-legged blacks. It can be filled with superbly fitting trap guns and long runs that are legends.

Here we can always have the right size shot and the perfect choke. Our quail will hold for our sculpture-solid pointer, and rights-and-lefts for us will be a matter of course. This is the place where the old $50 gun discovered at the antique store will be either a Purdey, a Boss, or at least a highly embellished Greener.

If we want an old dog to come back for an hour or so from wherever old dogs live forever, all we have to do is ask. We can be 11 again and fishing with untarnished wonder and a Prince Albert tin full of worms in our overall pocket.

Hill Country is the place we've never been or the place we always wanted to go back to. It can be a day we'll never forget or a day we've always dreamed would come to pass.

We can walk in the rain, sit in the sun, or huddle around the fire . . . whatever seems to be just right at the time. And we'll talk about the secret things that keep us coming back: the words we hear when the loons cry; the things we feel when the old dog falls asleep with her head laid lovingly across our knee.

All Hill Country needs is a few good friends to keep us company on our wanderings. I hope you'll come along and share it.

BIRDS OF A FEATHER

A successful duck hunter has to learn to think like a duck. It helps, of course, if he can talk like one, but it's more important to understand their philosophy and general outlook.

In order to cope with mallard, let's say, we have to come to appreciate their social structure. My attitude is, like most of my opinions, open to discussion and questioning—but as far as the mallard is concerned, here it is, for better or worse. The mallard is basically a Republican. Slightly on the conservative side, he wants less government and lower taxes. He tends toward the tenets of the Methodist Church, but would not object too strongly to a cocktail or a dance tune. He enjoys conventions, good stories, likes to brag a little and show off in front of the ladies. In short, the mallard closely resembles most duck hunters—so now we know to a large degree why he is their favorite duck; a good example of the old truism of "Like attracts like."

Let me give you a typical example of an avid mallard hunter, a friend of mine who works for one of the large gun companies. Last fall he immediately telephoned me when he returned from a trip to Stuttgart, Arkansas. I believe he used the word *unbelievable* about 15 times in the first minute. He used it to describe the country, the local people, his guides, the calling, the pin oak flats, and the number of ducks.

I listened patiently while he gave me a half-minute rendition of the feeding chuckle he'd learned on his visit. I admitted to envy on all counts, including his use of the call. After he'd calmed down a little, I, always curious, asked him about the use of decoys. "Didn't need 'em," he bragged and went on to tell me again, and in minute detail, about the "unbelievable" skill of the local guides with a duck call. "Tell me how you and the guides were dressed," I said, suddenly struck by a powerful intuition. He thought for a second or two and then told me what I had already surmised. "Well," he said, "I had on a green hat, a white scarf because it was chilly, sort of a grayish-green hunting coat, and those old sort-of-yellowish orange boots."

"Is that what the guides wore, more or less?" I asked. "You bet," he answered—and then the picture struck him as well: they were all dressed like huge, pot-bellied drakes. Each one a living decoy, of sorts; proving my point that this is the sort of thing you can expect from the truly dedicated gunner.

By now, I'm sure, you're thinking of other hunters and how they subconsciously have come to resemble, one way or another, a facet of their favorite sport. Pheasant hunters tend to talk a lot, dress in gaudy colors, and have excitable temperaments. They like to wear hats with a lot of pins on them and red bandannas around their necks.

Grouse dedicants, as we have long known, favor tweeds in russet shades. They are pipe smokers, serious thinkers, and tend to be on the quiet side. Their idea of a funny story is involved with dry wit or a fine turn of phrase.

Note, if you will, the curious head-turning movements of the woodcock fancier. His short fluttery movements as he rises to refresh your glass. How he subconsciously seeks the shady side of the street, and his uncanny ability to stand motionless for so long a time that he appears to have fallen asleep.

Even their wives, after some years of total exposure, will fall into the same patterns. A woodcock hunter's wife is often bigger than he is and tends to lead him around—even to the point of opening the door for him and cooking a lot of spaghetti. Mallard hunters' wives are chatty and tend to like parties with a lot of similar ladies. They snack a lot on cocktail tidbits and often talk with their mouths full.

The list of personal peculiarities is virtually endless—if you're afflicted with a sense of humor and a parallel curiosity. At any gathering of shooters, say a cocktail party or a D.U. dinner, you could make book that a group of five men standing together talking into each others' right ear and trying to trade shotguns are serious trapshooters. Retriever field-trial enthusiasts are the easiest—they are always covered with black hair, make wide, sweeping gestures, and shout a lot from slightly bent-over positions. Pointer and setter trialers are tough to separate. Both speak in hoarse whispers, their vocal cords having been long since worn out. They crouch a lot from years of imitating points, and they never wear blue serge suits. Their wives tend to go to the bathroom a lot, because they never know when they'll see indoor plumbing again.

When you stop to think about it, hopefully with kindness and understanding, you'll accept the fact that a lifetime of trying to match wits with small birds, a variety of dogs, and the occasional clay target—and knowing deep down inside that you'll never really succeed—tends to create what we might generously term idiosyncrasies. It leads us, as we have seen, into a life-style of protective coloration, philosophical identity with similar men and women, and a common language.

I feel very pleased knowing that many giant corporation presidents, Members of Congress, famous doctors and lawyers, celebrated movie stars, and the like share the same passions and frustrations to no less degree than the rest of us. I am warmed by certain knowledge that in high places as well as low, guns are traded, feeding calls practiced, hat badges cherished, russet tweeds are patched and mended and treasured. Both mansion and farmhouse closets alike hold their share of yellowish-orange boots and good suits covered with dog hair.

When the day comes that I am "looking natural," as they say, and they decide to go with my one good suit, I trust it will have a few muddy paw prints on it and that everybody will understand that if it were any other way I would feel very uncomfortable.

HUNTING THE HIGH COUNTRY

"I like feeling so close to the stars" is the reason a man gave when I asked him why he liked hunting the high country. But as we spent more time together in the mountains, I began to realize that what he said was not what he meant. Philosophers have long known that a man often laughs loudest at what he's most afraid of—and men often brag or boast about something that leaves them fearful or ashamed.

An old intellectual pun says, "It's no accident that so many mountain climbers are killed." And a weak parallel might be made that the tremendous lure of the stark and forbidding peaks is often based on an even greater feeling of dissatisfaction with the inescapable day-to-day problems and what passes for civilization. Many of the old mountain men were not so much drawn to the "freedom" of their way of life as they were repelled by what they were leaving. I think the "other side of the mountain" is more often not the one you turn your face toward—but the one you turn your back on. Perhaps we hunt the high country not to "see what we can see" but to find out what we can forget; a small escape from what some call *life* to what we call *living*.

Mountains, some say, are there like ideals and dreams, to give us a better perspective on our rather ordinary lives and hopes. Teddy Roosevelt said that he liked to go out at night and stare at the stars until he felt small again.

I like to walk in the mountains until I feel strong again. The first few days are the fearful ones of the stranger in an area of the unknown. Then, as the feeling of familiarity and physical power comes, we become more assured of our ability to exist along our part of the roof of the earth. The life we left behind comes to be seen as it is. Things fall into their right perspective. We come to know that we have climbed above that part of our lives that made us uncomfortable and sometimes sad by its smallness.

It may be the element of survival that holds such strong appeal. Not survival in the sense of holding on to life against natural forces that can easily destroy us—the cold and wild that lie in wait for the careless or the unlucky—but survival within the moral boundaries we know and believe in as a "rightness of things." A recapturing of some basic honesty about ourselves that is so easily lost in our day-to-day making a living. A basic feeling of happiness that we too often, and for too long, let lie fallow because it doesn't seem fitting or comfortable in a routine bordered by one small crisis after another.

But trade those "death and taxes" in for a week or so of making do in the mountains and watch them shrink back to the small size they really deserve.

I find it hard to imagine a symphony more evocative than the night sounds a man can hear in a high-country camp. The soft shuffle of a hobbled horse. The slapping crack of a beaver's tail as he works against the coming of the stone-cold freeze. The protesting of ancient trees against the winds probing them for mortal weaknesses, like old men whose thin voices betray the words that say "I'm fine." A swollen-necked elk bugling for one reason, and a coyote moaning complaints to the moon for another; and between them always flies the owl who best conducts his business in silence.

You just lie there and listen. And after a few nights of this, you begin to become deeply conscious of all the things going on—the elemental tides that flow as strongly as they did a million years ago. The night sounds tell of searches for survival, the testing of strengths and wills and cunning. You lie there and listen. And you know that after this your nights will not be quite the same. You lie there and listen. You hear the night noises a little differently now, and suddenly the things that brought you here in the first place— the things you were afraid of in your life down below—are not unconquerable fears, but just other noises in another kind of night. And then you lie there and sleep.

I like the sound of the phrase "high country." I like the threatening feel of its wind that sharpens our elemental instincts and cuts away the unimportant trappings that have driven us when we didn't want to be driven.

I like the smell of the pines and the glisten of the aspens. I like the quiet that makes the crack of a twig sound like a thunderclap.

I like to watch an old muley buck sneaking along the edge of the timber—feeling smug that he's outsmarted me—and me feeling smug because he hasn't, and letting him go along about his business.

But most of all, I like the feeling of being there just with myself. One of the old poets said "never less alone than when alone." And I don't know of a place that fits that more than sitting by yourself in the high country. Just looking down into the valleys and thinking.

I know now, or believe I do—which is about the same thing—why the old bulls like the dark corners of the mountains. They like to get away and think; to remember what it was like to be young and strong and knocking a tree over just for the hell of it— and maybe to show off a little, for the ladies.

My days of knocking things over and showing off a bit for the ladies are behind me. But now and then I like to remember the long ago time when the young girls called my name—and sitting in a place out of the wind, close to the blue sky in the high country, is as good a place as any.

ANNUAL REPORT I

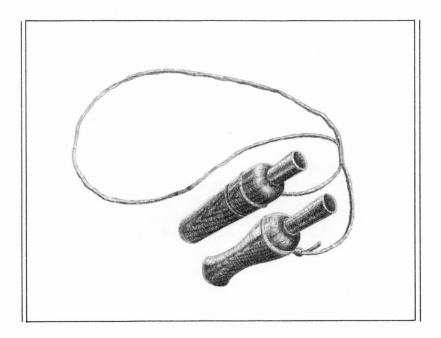

[Sound of applause.] Thank you, ladies and gentlemen. I'm honored to be here with my Annual Report. I think you'll realize that I haven't taken my responsibilities lightly and that the most important items are covered.

Like most years, this one past has been mixed. I believe that triumphs outweigh the tragedies, and, on balance, the report is rather pleasant.

First off, the goose that was born last year with the crippled leg managed to find a mate that appreciated her other qualities and returned to the pond and gave us five beautiful new Canadas.

The whitetail buck that lives in the cedar swamp has matured to a superb ten-pointer. But I'm afraid that his manners have not kept pace. He still leads his herd through 20 acres of standing field corn to get to the backyard vegetable garden, and they have ruined our stand of milk-and-sugar sweet corn, eaten all the lettuce, and generally left the whole patch in shambles.

The great horned owl raised at least three owlets that I could see in the hollow of the sycamore tree, so I suspect that our nightly serenades will continue on through the winter as usual.

Mallard frequent the pond in increasing numbers, and the pair of ospreys were back again this year, but the great blue heron did not return. I suspect the geese chased him off, but that may only be an optimistic speculation.

An investment was made for the future by taking one of the girls, Jennifer, to the Orvis Fly-Fishing School. I expect this to be a high-cost factor for the near future—a good number of my flies are already missing—but with any persistence on my part she may learn to tie her own, and we may yet end up with more than our original investment; but, to be honest, that remains another optimistic speculation at the present time.

One or two guns have been traded. One for a pair of fly rods, the other for the basis of upgrading our supply of trap guns. A new trap barrel (32 inches) has been acquired for the old Krieghoff, and we sincerely expect that to show immediate dividends. I realize that the same statement was made last year and proved to be disappointing, but this year is sure to be different.

We are also considering the acquisition of a new Winchester skeet gun, and a new three-inch Remington 1100 on the basis of steel shot being required in our favorite duck and goose locations. The Chairman of the Board is attempting to divert some of this proposed expenditure for a new screen door and a roof gutter over the kitchen window, but I'm confident that matters will be seen in their true measure and the right decisions made in the end. After all, we have lived without a screen door or roof gutter for the past eight years, and I can see no real necessity for their acquisition this close to the shooting season, and causing a major disruption in our carefully thought-out plans.

Three good pipes were lost by driving off with them resting on the top of the car and will have to be replaced. Two pairs of shoes were eaten by Josephine, the new Labrador puppy, and will also have to be replaced. (This expense will be borne by me personally since the Chairman is on record about my leaving my shoes around on the floor where Josephine could get at them.)

Other capital losses were fairly minimal. Small change in the poker game at the gun club, a side bet on the outcome of a shoot-off I was fortunate enough to be in, a box of trout flies dropped in the river and unnoticed at the time, a small side bet on how many salmon I would take on a fishing trip in New Brunswick (the number that won the pool was zero), another small side bet on how many ducks I could take with six shells (the number will remain confidential), and a small side bet on the weight of a largemouth bass I caught in Texas. With the past year still strongly in mind, small side bets in the coming year will be more carefully appraised.

I'm afraid that the shaggy-bark hickory by the pond was struck twice by lightning and will eventually have to be cut down, but the wood will be utilized in the big fireplace, hopefully for grilling venison steaks and surely for comfort while discussing why there is no venison, should that be the case. I should mention here that a black iron kettle to be used in the fireplace for making hot toddies is also under consideration, the health and well-being of my associates being of primary importance.

A canoe paddle and one sneaker were also lost last year in an incident that the Chairman finds unreasonably humorous—so I will not bore you with further details. She will undoubtedly discuss it at the smallest suggestion, as she has repeatedly all year, complete with grossly exaggerated gestures.

Concurrent with the canoe incident, a decision never again to be without a wading staff while stream fishing has been made. Why these things strike the Chairman as funny escapes me and gives rise to occasional doubts about her true concern for my comfort and safety.

None of our woodcock or grouse covers has been notably depleted. There are substantial reasons for this, which I'll be glad to go into with you on an individual basis. But at the bottom of this is my well-known tendency to offer the easier shots to my gunning companions and my experimentation with variations of the swing-through method of lead. Since I am through experimenting, I expect to be able to project a game dinner or two during the coming season.

That about covers our business of the Annual Report. I expect the ladies are anxious to return to their mending of heavy socks and the dubbing of hunting boots and the men are ready for a refreshment. I had planned to end the meeting with my rendition of the feeding chatter, but it seems that I've left my call in my other coat, along with my scores at trap and skeet.

I trust you will assume their superiority [sound of hisses and boos] and I wish you a season of fine days and close friends to share them. Again, I'm sorry I forgot my call.

[Sounds of hurried scuffling and sighs of relief.]

A GIFT OF LOVE

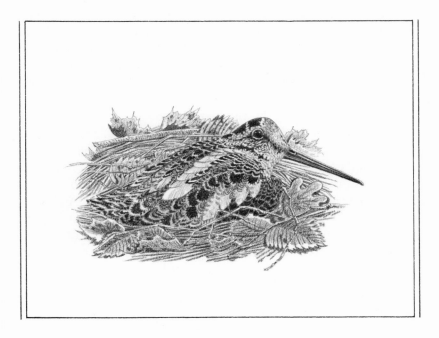

The beginnings of November are "the stuff that dreams are made on." But the mind's luscious idlings of discovery of new and secret covers seldom find reality in fact. However often we may see ourselves as the children of Boone or Clark, pioneering some small unknown, it almost never comes to be. Somehow or other our boots seem to find a more familiar path and our eyes look for places we've come to know and understand. A certain nest of popple, a friendly orchard, are homes where we find a special breed of friend. Year after year a woodcock flutters from the same old bog. The apple yields a grouse and just past the solid-rusted hay rake is an eight-bird covey.

There's no taking any glory from the outdoors pioneer, but what a thread to hold again by knowing that an ancient chestnut log that is now a deer stand for your son has yielded white-tailed bucks for you, your father, and his father before him. When the land-marks go they take the history of the land with them, and the ghosts of all the men gone before must find us in another place.

I know a lot of men who had nothing else to give their boys except a homemade blind at a kettle pond and an evening flight. How proud they were to sort of stand aside and let the young man shoot—all by himself, and take or miss as fate would have it. Before the flight and after, they would talk, these hard-wrought men whose tools were hands, not words.

Yet in the evening by the kettle pond they'd try to tell their sons what all this meant. Let there be no doubt that this was their greatest act of love. They'd talk about the clouds and how one meant rain and one foretold of coming snow. How this tree grew and what the bass were dimpling at. The words were few but warm, and carried meaning far beyond the simple act of talk. And then, suddenly, you were a man when you could go to the kettle pond yourself. It was just that simple—and just that profound. I can't think of a better place for a man to meet his son—or find him-self—than in a homemade blind by a kettle pond.

We all have our chestnut logs and blinds and orchards some-where in our past. And somehow if the deer we see is just a ghost and the partridge just a shadow in the leaves and a rustling of the wind, no matter; the knowledge that they once were here and cer-tain things were done and said is rich enough. They can never take away from us the place or two where always time stands still.

A LITTLE LOST

One of the things a lot of us can look forward to this fall is getting lost. The only reason I don't get lost a lot more than I do is that, like most people who spend most of their time hunting birds, the opportunity just doesn't present itself.

I must admit that I kind of like getting a little lost. It's always an adventure I hadn't counted on—a thrilling challenge that, in the wildest stretches of my imagination, puts my life in the balance. At the first moment of recognition (or really nonrecognition) is the exciting possibility that after all these years I'll finally get to use my secret waterproof match case and the candle stub. My emergency rations are usually shared with the dog at lunch, but I always have the beginnings of a fire and, depending on what hunting coat I'm wearing, a half-decent knife and maybe the little wire saw someone once gave me. My real emergency stuff is usually in the trunk of the car where I'll never need it or can't get at it.

If I could choose somebody to get lost with (excepting Ann-Margret, of course) it would have to be Jim Rikhoff. I spent the evening at his house while he was preparing for a pack trip into British Columbia for Stone sheep. The spare room was laid out with his gear. And I mean laid out wall to wall! There were at least two of everything I had ever read about and, in several cases, three of everything. There were huge piles of equipment featuring things I'd never even heard about and wouldn't know how to use if I knew what they were to be used for.

For example, Jim, who doesn't smoke, had a pile of three lighters, a pint can of lighter fuel and extra flints, a metal match gadget, a waterproof match safe for kitchen matches, and a small metal reflector he said was a solar lighter! There were enough boxes of Super-X.270 ammunition to storm Omaha Beach and enough clothes to have amounted to a six-months outlay of the Woolrich Mills.

I asked him what in the name did he need all this stuff for? He said that in that part of the country at this time of the year you never knew what the weather would be, and I said "Jim, I don't care where you're going, there just ain't that much weather *anywhere.*"

I kidded him pretty heavy but he's my boy in an emergency. I'll bet that not only does he have eight pairs of different kinds of pants with him but I'll bet they come in four different sizes. I imagine that the overweight charges on the plane would be enough to buy a new car, but Jim is not going to be one of those guys who in the middle of nowhere says "Boy, I wish I'd brought my ————." Whatever it is, Rikhoff will have it, in various colors and textures. When you see a guy like this preparing for a pack trip you thank your lucky stars you weren't born a horse. And I can't imagine Jim ever getting lost anyway. When you stagger off carrying as much stuff as he lugs, you just can't walk far enough to even get confused. He may get a hernia but he won't get lost.

Of course, there are all the little jokes about getting lost and what to do. You remember the one that says just start to make a dry martini and eight people will show up and tell you you're doing it wrong. Or the old Air Force adage that says when you're lost don't start walking along a railroad track or you'll be hit by a low-flying Navy pilot.

I had a long lecture one afternoon from a friend who is a navigational nut. He's read every book ever written on the subject and talks about his astrolabe with the same fervor a marine would use in describing a date with Miss America. He dwelt on the fact that the North Star is the one unvarying, constant thing in the heavens and one never need fear because you could do this and that. The difference, never expressed of course, is that he has a mind like a logarithm chart and the memory of an elephant, while I don't. I can never find the North Star because I can't find the Big Dipper and the Pointer stars, and if by some luck I did find it it would be meaningless because after that I'm zero on anything else.

It is just a lot simpler for people like me to accept the absolute certainty of someday being lost and prepare for it. I will dig out my emergency gear (mostly extra tobacco, matches, and pipe cleaners), try to build my fire, and stand right under what may or may not be the North Star and wait for somebody smarter to come and find me.

GOOD INTENTIONS

It's funny how often your good intentions turn out the very opposite of the way you expected. My good friend Angus Cameron was kind enough to ask me to share his goose blind with him for a day or so last fall and, through my usual combination of a lot of spent shells and some unwary birds, I finally had my geese.

Now Angus knows my wife and was commenting on what a nice job she was doing and how happy she was to be reshingling the garage roof while he and I were hard at work in the chill fields doing our damndest to put meat on the table. It then occurred to him that we ought to stop by a place that picks your geese for you so I could come home with nothing left for her to do with the birds but more or less pop them in the oven.

Well, unthinkingly, that's exactly what I did. I arrived home fairly late and my wife was in the kitchen waiting for me (in case I wanted a late snack or a drink). I wanted both and when she'd fixed them and I was eating she said, "Well, I might as well get started picking the birds," and began to lay out some newspaper to put the feathers on.

"No need for that," I told her, "I found a place that picks the birds and freezes them. It's all done for you."

The minute I said it, I knew I'd made a mistake. She almost started to cry—and I remembered that in 15 years of marriage I'd never shot a bird that she hadn't picked, and she counted on doing it.

"Where are the bushels of oysters you always bring home for me to shuck?" she asked me next, and I admitted that with the roofing I hadn't thought she'd have time—and that right after the shingling was done I'd promised her that she could paint the dog kennel. And I thought that after that was done she ought to take it a little easy and just loll around in bed mornings until 5 o'clock instead of getting up so early.

She didn't say anything, just made me another drink, lit her lantern, and went out to the car and brought in my hip boots and my shotgun. I watched as she stripped my 1100 Remington and began carefully cleaning it, as is her habit. (She always cleans the guns before she cleans the boots, especially if I've been out near salt water. I suppose a lot of wives do it the other way around—it's just what they're used to.)

"I'll bet Angus didn't take his birds to any commercial picker," she said in the same tone of voice women use when they ask you if you still love them.

"I don't know for sure," I said. "Angus is a real gentleman," she went on. "He told me that he lets his wife make all his hunting shirts, weave his minnow seines, tan the deer hides—that all a woman asks is to be allowed to do some little things to help out while the men are busy shooting and telling stories in front of the fire."

I admitted that Angus was probably a more thoughtful husband than I was and apologized again for at least not bringing a bushel of crabs for her to shell. As she finished the shotgun, using her toothbrush to clean out the checkering and putting a little Linspeed on a scratch in the stock, I was desperately trying to think of something that would make amends about the geese.

I thought of making a hole in one of my boots so she'd have something to patch, but by now she was just about ready to wash them off and vacuum the insides in case some twigs or leaves had gotten in that might cause me some slight discomfort. When she shut off the vacuum, I started chatting about the fun she could have come spring . . . she could start up her worm farm again in case Ernie Schwiebert came by and wanted to do a little fishing in the brook.

Then she interrupted me and I asked her what was the matter. She said, "Don't you notice anything different about me?" I looked blank and she gave me a hint. "It's something I'm wearing." And then I noticed she had on a sweatshirt that had some kind of a symbol on it and the words WOMEN'S LIB. I asked her what in the world did she want that for, hadn't I always treated her fair and square . . . especially when it came to work? "Why last year I even let you use my snow shovel," I reminded her.

She came over, laughing, and kissed my cheek. "That's not it, silly," she said. "I bought that for when you go trap shooting . . . don't you get it?" I admitted I didn't.

"Now all you have to do," she smiled, "is turn around and look at me and you'll remember."

"Remember what?" I asked.

"Don't you know what L-I-B should remind you of?"

I shook my head again, and she said, *"Lead It, Baby!"*

I thought it was such a great idea that I offered to give her back the money she'd spent on it. "Don't do that, you'll need it," she smiled. "When I cleaned out your hunting coat I noticed you were getting a little low on magnum 4s."

TEXAS DIGEST

I spent quite a lot of time in Texas this year, and I thought you might like a report on what's going on. First, there's good news—Texans are beginning to drink wine with their meals. That's right, straight wine; not mixed with a cola or anything!

This is a great aid to the average Easterner's digestion, which is as delicate as a hummingbird's when compared to a Texan's. Generations of Texas fathers have passed to generations of Texas sons an intestinal system like the maw of a snapping turtle. This incredible heredity gives them the ability to stop at a roadside cafe with a sign that proclaims EATS, and run from the pickup to a snack that covers chicken, fried steak, Mexican hot sauces, raw onions, hot ketchup, and *jalapeño* peppers, all topped off with a piece of plastic pie, ice cream, and a handful of corn chips.

I'm not saying that Texas food isn't tasty, or possibly even nourishing; it's just that I can't hit the average truck stop there without the same feeling I had when I boxed—I know I'm going to get hurt, it's only a question of how bad.

But I'm learning. For dessert I pass up the fluorescent orange pie and have a dollar's worth of antacids instead.

A Texas public eatery is basically judged by the jars of chili peppers, banana peppers, and a variety of commercial and home-made sauces that are hot enough to weld steel. Food of the common variety, beef or chicken, is merely used as a carrier for the hot stuff. If a man entering one of these establishments sees six or more acid-proof laboratory jars on each table, plus a huge supply of cold beer, then starts to salivate like Pavlov's dog—he's a sure-enough Texan. If tears come to his eyes, it's me.

Naturally the only thing a Texan eats when he hits a fancy place with his wife of an evening is steak. His wife eats the same thing, only hers is less than two pounds. And it can only be ordered rare. I've tried medium and well done, but the well-done order almost got the chef out of the kitchen in a rage. They serve it to me rare anyway; the specifying is merely an imitation of an Eastern formality. A rare Texas steak is about a foot in diameter, three inches thick, and is minus the hide. There is absolutely no way a cook can ruin it, because he doesn't do anything more to it than sling it under a broiler long enough to get it over room temperature. I've seen animals hurt worse get well.

Texans also eat Mexican food, which I am told is delicious. It's a moving sight to see a 240-pound, six-foot-four man with banana-sized fingers cradling a taco like a jeweler holding a ruby. He tastes it and then invariably adds some juice from one of the little laboratory bottles on the table. He tastes again and adds more juice. Only when little blisters appear on his lips and moisture seeps through his hatband is he satisfied. A voice barely above a whisper creeps through his tortured throat—"Is that *good!* Best Mexican restaurant for a hundred miles!" Now what the restaurant has offered him beyond a jar of paralyzing pepper concoction that I'm afraid to smoke near is beyond me. You could dunk a breadstick in it and get the same end result. Why the traditional toothpick doesn't go up in flames is a mystery.

Texans are as proud of their food as they are of everything else. There's no doubt in my mind that there have been more fights over what makes a proper chili or barbecue than there have been over the War between the States. There's also no doubt that I have not partaken of either *proper* chili or barbecue; otherwise I wouldn't be writing this piece—I'd be in some gastrointestinal ward, wired up like a moon shot.

I must say that there is no one on earth who is fonder of Texas and Texans than I am. I'd rather have a gall bladder attack in Fort Worth than a perfect pressed duck in Paris. And it's odds-on, anyway.

I believe that Texas food rises to its heights in a hunting camp. It starts off with a cold cola to deaden what's left of the stomach lining. Then comes vension sausage made with 50 percent meat and 50 percent of ingredients that would not get in the front door of the FDA. I do know that you mix up the components while wearing asbestos barbecue gloves. This is followed by the Mexican touch: *huevos rancheros.* These are several eggs covered by a fire-colored sauce whose constituents are, or should be, listed in the San Antonio Poison Control Center. This is all washed down by either more cola or what is called coffee. The coffee isn't really thick enough to patch a driveway; it's more the consistency of drilling slurry. If you're strong, you can stir it enough to dissolve some sugar. Don't bother to add milk or cream: it won't mix. I once drank half a cup and it left a stain on my teeth for a week. It took a whole plug of Cannonball to take the taste out of my mouth.

Lunch is chili. The average Texan must eat chili at least twice a week or he suffers an attack of digestion. I gather that real chili doesn't have beans in it, and I think I know why: a bean takes up the space that they would rather have occupied by tiny flakes of an assortment of lethal peppers. You have to be careful with chili, because if you spill any, it eats a hole in your blue jeans. If you drink about eight ounces of beer to two ounces of chili, you ought to be about right. It's a must to say that you like it—if you can't talk, at least nod your head and smile.

Supper is always steak. If you're lucky and it's cooked over a campfire, you can keep tossing it back until it gets cooked. Try to be subtle. Texans think that well-done steak is part of the International Communist Conspiracy.

I've been with some of my Texas friends in one of the world's most famous restaurants and watched them cold-eye a meal that included an exquisite truffled Strasbourg pâté, Dover sole poached in a delicate white wine, and a veal *piccata* that would bring tears to the eyes of Escoffier, the way a four-year-old would disdain a double order of spinach. They eat it—but to them it ain't *food.*

But as I said, I consider myself an adopted Texan. It's one of the few places in the world that I hate to leave and can't wait to get back to. If I ever meet you in Texas, let's just shake hands and say "Howdy." Please don't take me to lunch at a place with a sign that says EATS.

WHEN IT ALL BEGINS AGAIN

I'll bet you first learned to whistle in the spring. That's what spring is all about—a time to begin things. A time to do something new, to try something different. The time to learn to whistle, the time to learn to throw a fly or tie one. The time to go buy a new rod, different lures, and to think about new places. The time to break in a new hat, or repaint the boat.

It's time to look up some old friends—that big bass by the spring run, the perch off the rocks, the pickerel that lives by the dock. Or make some new ones—the surf-running stripers, the blue-water marlin, tidewater redfish, or gulf-water dolphins.

Fish little for shellcrackers and crappies. Fish big for muskies or northerns. Take a nap by the brook, or roar around with twin "50s." Do whatever you like—that's what I like about fishing . . . and fishermen.

If your year begins with the first wet line—you're a fisherman. If you tuck away a pail of shiners behind a 20-pound tackle box—you're a fisherman. If pork rind smells like perfume and moonlight reminds you to try poppers—you're a fisherman. If you remember the date and weight of your big one—and forget your wife's birthday—you're a fisherman. And if you'll fish in a storm and won't mow the lawn in a mist—I'll bet you learned to whistle in the spring.

Right now it's beginning time. The world is new again, and everything is waiting. It's time to say "Get the skillet out, honey, I'm going fishing." If you hope this is the year that they'll be bigger and more of them (and really don't care), you're a fisherman. And I'm a fisherman too.

JUST RIGHT

Right about now the deer are teaching this year's fawns how to sneak under my garden fence. The Canadas that honeymooned under the black pine on the island in my pond are scolding their handful of goslings for coming too close to me when I'm out practice fly casting. (I'm not sure whether this comes from an aesthetic point of view or just parental concern.) The big bass that nested in the muskrat burrow is rolling at minnows, and the Labradors are digging the first of their summer dusting holes under the boxwood by the kennel. I'm just plain loafing—being happy watching and knowing that 100 years ago, and in 100 years to come, just about exactly the same things will be going on. The place might be different, the featured players will not be the same, but someone just like me will be watching the coming of summer and thinking that the world is full of good things.

The womenfolk might think I'm idle, but I'm really not. I'm storing up pictures in my mind against hard times. There will surely come a day when I'll need to see a string of little geese to make me feel more certain about what I ought to believe in. And worrying about the deer tracks along the lettuce rows helps to take my mind off larger problems for at least a little while.

No matter where I am, I can always see a buttonball of mallard duckling worrying a dragonfly, or a sulking rainbow asking a question that I never answered. I can see a woman and remember a young girl proudly skinning her first muskrat. Or I'll observe a graying dog and think up a puppy with a stolen shoe.

Our good things, in my belief, are meant to last. And I'm always sorry about the ones who see my mounted fish or the weather-whitened deer horns on the barn and miscalculate as to why I keep such things. They seem to think it's size or shape or vanity or that I'm showing off. And you know it's not that way at all. My modest brook trout is, in truth, a week of fishing in the wilderness with a very favorite long-time friend. It's not the fish itself I've saved, but the pictures that it calls to mind—canoes, caribou, and warm beer lunches on a huge flat rock that felt as soft as hay and as warm as gold at noon. I'm not even sure which one of us it was who caught that trout—nor do I care. Our greatest trophies are not things, but times.

About the deer horns, I remember very well. They're there because of a country kitchen with a wood cookstove and the smell of pancakes and the excitement and the laughter and the men kidding you to let you know they knew you could be trusted to hunt with them at last. And they're there because of a mother who, not quite so sure about the growing up, put a special sandwich in your pocket—instead of the kiss she could give yesterday's schoolboy but not this morning's hunter.

The place where I got that buck is covered with a house today, but the memory is powerful enough to make it disappear when I drive by, and all I have to do to smell pancakes and see Mom is to wait a minute by the side of the road.

No doubt at all that you have a duck or covey spot or willow that once sheltered a bass that's as fresh in your mind—and still as close to reality—as the minute it all happened. And no doubt you'll leave these things to someone else as little memories of what you loved and who you are and why. I don't believe that my girls ever thought it wrong or strange for me to stop and say, "Right there by that crabapple tree is where I saw the woodcock pulling worms." Nor do they ever ask, "What woodcock?" They have always known that it was a special woodcock; a bird that they can still see, years later, as plainly as I saw him then. And we always hope that someday we'll see another one, right there, but almost never does it turn out just the way we would like it to be.

But I know that there will always be new bass, new fly rods, new geese and puppies, new trap guns, new shells, and a fresh start. When you look at the world in the coming of summer and how much of it is shining-new, you ought to loaf a minute, drink it in, and say to yourself, "Just right."

Having things about which you can say, "Just right," is an attitude you create yourself—it's how *you* feel about things according to your sense of harmony. It's like the story of the Yankee farmer who gave his hired man a bottle of homemade applejack. The hired man took it with a nice New England blend of gratitude and skepticism, had a long pull, wiped his lips with the back of his hand, and said, "It's just right!"

"Just right, you say?" the farmer questioned. "So it is," the hired man replied. "If it was any better you wouldn't have give it to me and if it was any worse I couldn'a drunk it. Just right!"

TRASH OR TREASURES

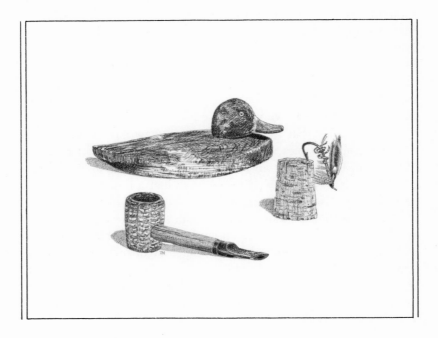

One of the older traditions I remember with mixed emotions is Spring Cleaning. The past year's gathering of household and farm stuff was gone over and weeded out in the process of making everything as clean and neat and functional as possible.

Kids were sized up and clothes were exchanged, or if past that stage put away in the attic for possible use as quilting material or stuff for rag rugs or something. I can hardly ever remember anything just plain thrown away; that is the one fact that has colored my own hoarding and stockpiling. I admit that my goods and chattels have neared the point that a nuclear physicist might call a "critical mass," but somehow I can find some excuse not to throw it away—condition, practicality, and common sense notwithstanding.

It's often an embarrassment when a nonhunting or fishing friend comes around and sees the accumulation. One of the piles that never fails to shock is the hip boots and waders. I don't bother to do much more explaining than "insulated" and "noninsulated" and point out that waders are higher than hippers. Never such details as felt soles, cleats, duck hunting as opposed to trout fishing— and since I don't bother with that you can be sure I won't mention that about three pair are completely worn out and for some reason I just can't bear to throw them out. There are a whole lot of people in this world who don't understand how a grown man with a college degree can get sentimental over a pair of rubber boots. So be it.

I'm sure that your basic list and mine vary just a little—maybe in size and color: hunting vests that haven't fit me since I was 14, shrunken wool caps, moth-eaten scarves, single gloves, rusty-bottomed tackle boxes, butchered gun stocks, odd pieces of leader material (questionable both in strength and size), flies with the hooks broken off on some forgotten streamside rock, empty .270 cases, jars of hardened stock varnish, miscellaneous and completely unlabeled gun parts, and on and on and on.

But a real saver, as opposed to the merely thrifty or future-minded, is readily identified by what even he will admit—if forced—is junk. And I am a junk saver. No . . . a junk protector. A Patron Saint of the wornout, rusted-through, unidentified, and unmendable. I once, at an auction, bought after the regular sale was long over what the auctioneer called the "contents of the barn." I remember opening the bid for $10 and raising my own, through the artifices of the auctioneer, to $11.

I don't know how long since you've been through a so-called empty barn on a once good-working farm, but it ain't empty—not by a truckload . . . or two.

I was standing there trying to figure out how I'd explain this to my wife when a man walked up to me and said, "What'll you take for that thing up on the wall?" I looked at it and said, "I don't know what it is . . . and if you want it you can have it." "It's a piece of a clutch for an old Fordson tractor, and I've been looking for one for years—I'll give you $3 for it." "Sold," I said. Anyway I stood there waiting for my wife and sold about $20 worth of stuff and still went home with a truckload. It so happens that I have a barn myself—and as the collectors' theory goes, if you have room for it, why not?

Along with the odds and ends that I can't identify, the stuff that *might* someday be useful is the junk that you think you'll create a use for. Old paint cans—someday you might want a boat anchor and all you have to do is pour a little cement, right? Railroad spikes—suppose you want to hang something heavy from a tree; they'll come in mighty handy. Odd lengths of chain—nobody *ever* throws away chain, it's immoral. Old tires—lots of possibilities there—dock bumpers, if I should ever have a dock, just to mention the only one I can possibly think of.

And what about old coats? Did you ever see an old barn that didn't have a blue jacket hanging from a rusty nail? You bet you didn't. Or a boxful of old spark plugs? Piles of old newspapers, a whiffletree, lock parts, handleless ax heads, hoes, shovels, picks, and heavy hammers; be as good as new when I get around to fixing them up.

Nothing is so forlorn or starveling as a barn without all these good things scattered around. And nothing so warms the heart of a barn owner as to be able to stir around and survey his treasures. Except for that most glorious of moments when someone says, "Say, you don't happen to have about three feet of one-and-a-quar-ter-inch galvanized pipe, do you?" And not only do you have it, but you can go right there and put your hands on it in less than an hour! The only thing that can top that is having an old pipe threader or cutter to show off with. Why your great-grandfather would think you turned out half-right after all if he could see you now.

Junk? Sure it is, I guess. But you can't help thinking that sometime, somewhere, for some reason it was needed. Somebody wanted it, bought it, or made it and used it to help him get along. So let's let it rest in our place, under the nests the mud-daubers and swallows make, in the corner behind the horse-drawn harrow, next to the plough with the sweat-stained handles.

Junk? Depends on how you look at it. One man's trash is an-other man's memory—his history, his link to the broad-backed men and their women who wrote little family notes on the pages of the front hall Bible. "Only an old rake?" Sure, but I can remember my father smoothing the rows in the kitchen garden with it—just to make it look neater and prettier.

A lot of people who aren't around any more wouldn't like it if

I threw their things out of the barn. I guess I don't really see these odds and ends as mine. I'm just holding them for the day when somebody needs something to make something else work . . . or to make something prettier. To soften a labor or add a flourish of pride and joy.

THE DAY THEY TOOK
MY GUNS

My Dear Grandchildren:

Today is the day they come to take my guns.

I thought I'd write something about the way I feel about it, because, being my grandchildren, you might otherwise never get a chance to know how much so many of us cared about our guns and how deeply they represented a precious part of our lives.

Of course, the hunting has long since disappeared. It wasn't too long after the so-called "humane societies" had seen to the end of gunning seasons that there were no more birds or animals to speak of. The white-tailed deer were about the first to almost disappear from a combination of overcrowding, disease, and starvation. After Ducks Unlimited was forced to close down, the breeding grounds were no longer cared for, and except for a few mallard crossbreeds and the odd farm-raised Canada goose, the skies were empty.

It seemed that once they got the hunting stopped that was all they cared about, and when the money that the hunters had contributed every year dried up so did the animals, and that was virtually the end of it. A lot of us had predicted what would happen—but we were voted out and that was that. It was like the end of a Crusade. Once the thing was over the people who felt they were righteous all forgot what the point of it was.

It seemed, as so many of us tried to say to the politicians, that the Brothers of Bambi and all the rest didn't really care about the animals themselves, all they wanted was the end of what they thought was cruel. Now they know what cruel is—or should.

Some of the gun clubs continued for a while, and a few of us stayed on to shoot a little trap and skeet, but somehow it wasn't the same. Crowds would come around and wave signs and carry on against us, and the simple pleasure of smelling a little powder and breaking a few clay targets was nationally shouted down as something akin to criminal.

Looking back on it, I can see how it all happened—I think. A lot still believe it was the growing criminal lobby that was at the bottom of it. And it turned out that it would be easier to stop the hunting seasons first and then make a play for the guns, than the other way around—which they had tried first.

I know you'll read about it in school, but I wanted you to hear the other side of it at least one time. You might get some idea when you see the pictures of me and your grandmother and friends with our bird dogs and retrievers.

We had some marvelous times together, especially down along the Eastern Shore. Back in the 1970s there were nearly a million geese there, and early in the season, fine flights of pintails, which were our favorites. (You ought to look up the pintail in one of your books to see what a beautiful bird it was.) And there were always the old standbys—the green-headed mallard. Somewhere in my stuff you'll find a couple of duck calls—you ought to save them. I suspect they'll be collectors' items before too long. The one that makes sort of a quack is the mallard call, which we used most—the others are goose calls, and I think I saved a couple of pintail whistles.

I don't suppose you can imagine a day with the dawn storming out of the northeast and all of us dressed in six layers of old clothes, the retrievers whining softly with excitement and us crouched down in the blind making soft clucks on the calls whenever a flock of birds seemed interested in our decoys.

We'd play a little game a lot—we'd talk about having roast duck or goose for supper, and we'd take turns picking something to go along with it. Your grandmother liked things like turnips and squash—she was a Yankee—and I liked things like greens and collards (you might have to look those up!). I guess that maybe all the fooling with guns and dogs and calls and decoys and the silly arguments over how to cook a duck or goose and was beach-plum jelly as good as cranberry don't amount to much—but things were simpler then, and we and our friends looked forward to those days as much as anything I can remember.

Well, I started to tell you about the guns. Mostly I had shotguns. But I had a few rifles that I loved and had carried many a mile from Alaska to Africa—and over quite a little country in between.

Some of my shotguns I thought were lovely—to me they were a form of art, and I liked to look at them almost as much as I liked to use them. Some were Italian, some English, some German, but most were made right here in the United States. Back when I did most of my bird hunting, we had any number of ducks and geese, as I said before, but also, right here in the East, if you can imagine it, we would go out after ruffed grouse and woodcock, English pheasant and quail. Most of the best quail hunting was down South, and we'd go there whenever we had a chance, and we always hoped to spend some time gunning doves. We'd argue about how to cook doves and quail, too, but no need to go into all that since I don't think you'd really understand how deeply this was a part of our lives. Our bird dogs were named Jag and Little Ben and Tippy and Judy Pup and Daisy and even one called George, because he looked like a friend who gave him to us. I know that doesn't mean much now either, but I just wanted you to know—for no particular reason except it's kind of important to me just to put their names on paper.

They used to tease me a lot about how much I loved the shotguns. I guess I had more than enough, since I had one (some said two) for about every kind of hunting. You didn't really need them all—but as I said, I liked them for a lot of reasons. There was even a time, long before they closed down the hunting, that we used to hang them on the wall the way you would a painting.

I guess there's no great sense of going into all that now since it doesn't mean much—just an old man meandering about something that he once loved very much, and that a part of his life went along with them on the day they took them away. I guess, to be honest, that all the songs and stories I like to remember best have come from the times spent with my friends in some gun club or hunting camp. But even to me all that is beginning to seem so very long ago.

The police are the ones that are coming to get the guns. I know they don't like that job much either, but since there are so many funny laws now I guess they just have to go ahead and do what they have to do.

I must let you in on a secret unlawful thing I did. I took the guns I liked best and buried them in the field behind the barn where I used to run the dogs on quail and woodcock and pheasant every now and then. I just couldn't stand the thought of having them melted down or thrown off a boat into the ocean. I saved a few to turn in, and I hope that does the trick. It seems that you can get away with a lot of pretty bad crimes, but if they catch an honest man with a gun that he hid away, out of sentiment, it goes pretty hard with him.

Well, they're all gone now. The young fellow that came for them was a State Trooper I used to shoot trap with every now and then. He looked through the stuff I handed over and didn't see my old favorite trap gun. It wasn't much to look at anyway—the checkering was smooth and the bluing pretty much worn away. And I think he took note that a few others weren't there either, but he didn't say a word. He's a nice young man, and as I say, just doing his duty. I suspect he saw the fresh dirt on my boots, and I suspect I saw a small tear or two when he put my little collection in his car. I'm not *sure* I did, but I hope so.

> With all my wishes that
> things may someday change,
> Your loving grandfather,
> Gene

MOST FAVORED OBJECTS

One of my favorite pastimes is rummaging around in my very assorted fishing tackle, untangling this from that and wishing for rods and reels that are beyond me—both in price and function. (I've always had a hankering for an old Payne or Gillum or Garrison rod, for instance, and once I was foolish enough to mention this in front of one of our more famous trouters with whom I'd fished once or twice. I knew that my casting and presentation made him wince, but I was a bit put back when he remarked that my having such a rod was like putting a pearl necklace on a hog.)

Anyway, my wife, just passing through, watched me hack at a piece of petrified pork rind I'd left for a year on a Johnson Silver Minnow and then go on separating the knot that plugs always seem to get into when left together for any time. "Why don't you get rid of some of that old rusted junk? And why don't you get yourself a new fly vest—the one you're using now is a mass of patches, it stinks, and the zippers are broken—just to mention the obvious."

She further remarked that she had better things to do than watch me play with my toys and went on about her business of cleaning out the gutters.

Nobody, hardly, takes his wife's comments about "fooling with toys" less seriously than I do, but she had set me to thinking about doing a little weeding out, and so I set to sorting the good from the bad from the indifferent.

I gingerly held up my old fly vest and had a good look at it. The pockets were filled with essentials carefully gathered over the years: folding cup, two partially rusted knives, a half paper of Edgeworth pipe tobacco, lead core line, various split-shot, useless matches, nonsticky bandages, an empty bottle of insect repellent (partly responsible for odor), part-empty bottle of fly flotant (partly responsible for stains), several flies with broken hooks, an assortment of hook hones, forceps, scissors, clippers, antacids, aspirin, tweezers, sunglasses, thermometers, half a bag of salted peanuts, pieces of leaders, spools of leader material, rain jacket, several red handkerchiefs, old licenses, line cleaner, muculin, pliers, an indeterminate sandwich, and a small plastic bottle containing about a half ounce of Scotch whiskey—which is still O.K. There were also several boxes of flies, wader patches, some plastic salmon eggs, and some small stones I had gathered from the bottoms of rivers like the Spey, Patapedia, Miramichi, Père Marquette, and the Au Sable, to ensure my return to these waters.

I more or less tidied everything up and put most of the things back. Fooling around with an old fishing vest is rather like robbing a grave. You are violating sacred ground. I realized that I was very partial to the way my vest smelled and looked. There is a point where one man's junk becomes another man's Most Favored Object.

My old fishing sweater was moved from the Bad pile to the Good. This too, now that I was remembering the times and places I'd worn it, was a Most Favored Object. My little Hardy reel that had been dropped and broken beyond repair carried a few memories as well; only an unfeeling accountant would have tossed it out as a total loss, so I put it up on the bookcase—along with a few other useless Most Favored Objects. I admit that this section of the bookshelf might qualify as a graveyard of derelict odds and ends to the casual observer—but to me they had earned the status of MFOs.

I don't know when something makes the magic transformation from useless to priceless, but I do know that most of us have a lot of them. Reedless duck calls, old dog licenses, compasses that don't know *N* from *S,* broken-bladed pocket knives, warped rods, headless decoys, faded pictures, puppy-chewed books, bits of leather, partridge and mallard feathers, single gloves, leaky boots, brittle and faded deer horns, old magazines—all MFOs, just to mention a few of the more common we have lying around.

I don't know exactly why it's so hard to part with so much of this sort of stuff. Maybe because so much of it was at one time deemed hard to come by and costly when a dollar an hour was good pay; some just plain and honestly worn out from years of decent service and deserving now to be cherished and honored. And various others saved, perhaps for the someday when we have the time, to be repaired and pressed back into function one more time. And, of course, we feel better for having them around; no real good reason—but as the kids at one time used to say, "Just because."

Well, at least I know there's lots of company. I have a friend who could buy me ten times over who shoots, by preference and affection, an old over-and-under that isn't fit to be a lamp. Another that spends more money keeping an old mid-30s Bentley running than almost any really fine car would cost brand new. And I know just exactly why they feel that way. Some things aren't really things at all, but friends, regardless of how cold they might be to the stranger's touch.

When you get down to thinking why you like the old faithful odds and ends so much, you begin to realize how much you've come to resist getting things that feel brand new. I hate to break in a new pipe, haircut, hunting coat, fishing vest, wool shirt, brush pants, or a leather belt.

I feel like a stranger in a new suit or with an unscratched shotgun or new boots. I'm at least tentative and cautious with plastic bass plugs and tackle boxes. I still miss silk lines, straight-handed casting rods, paper shotshells, and all-cotton shirts. I do not trust things that say "One size fits all"; I don't consider myself "all." I am me: a tried and true 16-35, 44 regular.

My skull has a series of strange contours, and the very thought of coping with a new hat gives me a headache. New sweaters are nearly as bad. It took time for me to be the shape I am; it will take time for my outer garments to get the hang of it.

I guess I like being surrounded with the impedimenta that have had the courage and integrity to stick with me, knowing how ill-adapted I am to care for things or, heaven forfend, to repair something. If a hunting coat doesn't rip or a pair of waders don't leak, I consider that a personal favor which I will return by hanging onto them—when they do eventually tear or split a seam, I feel honor bound to do my best to get my wife to set it right. That's the least a man can do for a Most Favored Object!

I'm coming to the time when I've got a lot of things that have needed a little repair personally. I still shed water and most of my seams are tight, but I like the air a little warmer when I hit the stream, and if I'm a little slow tying a fly on, I hope whoever's with me will wait a minute. Sooner or later, I know someone will have to judge me as Good, Bad, or Indifferent, and act accordingly. But maybe if they look into all my private pockets and see the things I've kept "just because," they might remember what I was, and why, and do the same for me.

A VERY SMALL PARADE

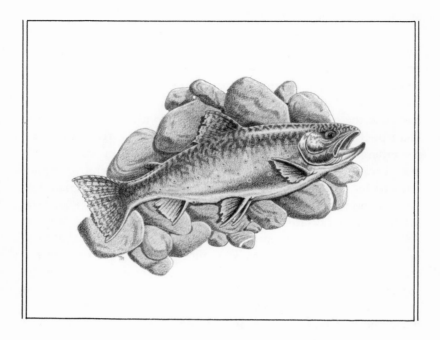

It is at night, with its common mix of inviting darkness and the things that wait for us behind the edge of sleep, when I most often look back at things that happened in the out-of-doors that I remember with deep pleasure—the things that I go out-of-doors to find and carry in my mind for just such times as these.

These are my treasures, and I like to count them out and shine them up. This is my savings book; one deposit a pair of pintails forever hooked above a spit of Manitoba marsh, another a rocking-chair mulie in a now-you-see-him, now-you-don't snow squall on an aspen-wrinkled Colorado hill. And so they can be paraded by, almost at will. A red-maned lion. An elephant so perfectly placed on a mountainside that I expect to go back there in years to come and find him standing just the same—pink-tinged in the sunset—as unchanged as a monument and as permanent in my mind. The white behind of an elk in black timber, the head turning back around, in a kind of comic double-take, when he realized he wasn't quite as alone as he thought . . . then, with all the dignity of a church elder, walking off as if to call me rude for stumbling, unannounced, into his private room.

A covey of quail drawn shoulder-to-shoulder in a circle as if carved in oak, believing, as I backed away, that I hadn't seen them.

I'm looking for a path to walk again; to come to find some soft and quiet place to rest. I want to listen to the gray shrikes calling in their flutelike pipings. Or stretch out in a Rocky Mountain meadow and wonder if the beaver that I'm watching ever dream or idly ponder any thoughts beyond their eternal sentence of rearranging their small brook.

I want to go beyond the everyday and find someplace else to be. I rummage again in my little storehouse. Past the lion (too fearful for now), beyond the elephant (too big to cope with), avoiding the elk, the deer, the quail, and come at last to just what I had been looking for all along.

A small boy I once had known, and even liked, arrived, wearing a straw hat (yes, I wore a straw hat) and carrying a fishing pole—an unknowing imitation of Young America at Play, complete with freckles and a mingled dog in tow.

And so, at the near edge of sleep, I joined this welcome, almost forgotten friend, and the two of us, as one, went back to better days.

Where should we go this day? Up the brook, of course. Its gentle banks lined with pussy willow and myrtle allowed no other choice for play. Up the brook meant barefooting it from stone to stone—to walk along the bank would be a travesty to being young and full of spring.

Where up the brook? Why to the Swimming Hole, of course. (Yes, I had a Swimming Hole, complete with a Big Rock to jump from.)

And then lying down, face bending the water as lightly as a skimming skater, I saw the trout that I had come to find.

Taking just the string in hand, I pushed the pole back on the rock and swam the threaded worm so gently toward the trout that he could not resist. And then, with a flip of the wrist, I flung him back to thrash surprised and frightened amidst the reluctant, sullen fragrance of the ferns.

The hook pulled free, and because of this, I think, I stood and watched to see which way he'd flop—like a speckled coin, tossing of its own free will. Toward the trees he's mine, and toward the brook he's free, I said—becoming a Solomon, trying on a life for size. So this little man watched the flip-flopping fish decide its life in random bendings.

My dog barked, from quite a safe distance, and almost as fearful that I would win as might I lose this awful game, I held his collar so he wouldn't interrupt my little play at being God.

I remember wondering could the fish know which way lay life or death? Would the game be long or short? And suddenly, he stilled and rested in the green. And then (instinct or chance? We never know) he came as close to sitting up as any fish I've ever seen and made straightaway for home.

Had he won or had I? No matter, really. But now I like to think I would have put him back no matter what. And then again, I'm not so sure. The prizes of youth in those early days were few and far between, and how hard it must have been to turn one back.

Either way, no matter now, except that I feel good remembering one spring, my Big Rock and my Swimming Hole and one fish, and looking tonight into the deeper dark I can see my trout still living there—and somehow sleep.

50-50 OR BUST!

I guess that I'm one of the most popular dove shooters in the country—as far as the doves are concerned. And the shotshell manufacturers. And the guys I shoot with in a shells-per-bird money pool.

But I know all about gunning them, nevertheless. I just know more than I can do. I can chat for hours on shot size, points of choke, swing-through, point-out, and sustained lead. And for dessert, go on to shadbellies, roachbellies, straight-hand, and finish up with the good points regarding a reverse Monte Carlo. If I could match wits with a dove, I'd fare fine, but, as it stands, I find a little trouble swinging while they swoosh. If you're the same way, smile; there are enough of us to vote the majority ticket.

You know what the ideal dove gun for any given day is? Your other gun—the one you left home in the closet. You can bet heavy money that on the day you have 24-karat confidence, and when by figuring out the wind, the feeding area, etc., etc., your vast experience tells you that today they'll be a mile high, and you load up on 7½s for your modified and full, you won't see a dove more than 23 yards away, unless it's 20 yards over another shooter. And needless to say, vice versa.

The genius-class dove shooter never does that. He always brings both guns. He says he's got an extra one because his regular gun tends to hang up once in a while, and the other's just a spare. The same guy carefully lets everyone see that he has only one box of shells. What they don't see is the three or four handfuls he's poured into the gun case; probably hand-loaded with two ounces of No. 8.

Really serious dove shooters are as dedicated as duck hunters and no more sane. One of my friends, who's avid for both, has trained his retriever to carry a cold six-pack out to the dove stand. Another is doing a probability study on a computer, about whether he's more likely to annoy an early-morning Arizona rattler if he's first in line walking across the field, in the middle, or bringing up the rear. (I favor the middle and take a lot of short steps.)

You can always tell a long-time dove gunner by the way he refuses certain shots. If he can't hit left angles, he always stands so that's where the sun bothers him, and he complains about the light all day. If he's got the magic touch on quartering birds and can't handle the straight-on incomers, he'll bring his gun up, swing through, and, without firing a shot, remark how it's a little too elementary for him to waste his skill on birds that fly right down the pipe.

The mean thing about dove shooting is that you're kind of "naked before your enemies." Everybody can see just what you've shot—or just shot *at*. And everybody will be more than delighted to keep tabs on your shooting, no matter how indifferent they tend to be on their own shooting arithmetic. If you ever have a simply spectacular day in the dove fields, I'll guarantee that you'll be out there alone with nothing more in the way of witnesses than a sleepy mule or a shuffling sow. Common sense dictates that such days are best kept quiet—no matter how strong the temptation to brag just a wee bit. You must remember that there are no "easy" shots at doves. Just when you think you've mastered the brutal left-to-right screamer, you're a sure bet to miss five in a row—ten if you've ever mentioned to your gunning buddies how nifty you are now on that particular bird, and they're in the field watching you for a demonstration.

I've been fortunate enough to have shot with some superb shotgunners, and I'd say that they are, by and large, believers in the swing-through school. They don't track their birds until the instant before they intend to shoot, then they bring the gun up, keeping their eyes on the bird, not the gun barrel, and with a very short and fast move come from behind the bird, establish their lead, and fire. If you remember the system, and trust it because it's true, your gun will follow your eye if you mount it properly and keep your head on the stock. A good trick that some top shooters use is to visualize the shot in your mind a second or so before you bring the gun up to make it. For example, if you see a bird that's going to be an incomer, you mentally "see" the gun coming up behind the bird, swing through, and just as you pass it, you shoot—keeping the barrel moving. Then as you actually shoot, you'll have a tendency to do what you've just rehearsed in your mind.

If there is one outstanding fault of the poor shooter, it has to be stopping the gun the moment he fires. The truly fine shots all agree that nothing is more important than a consistent and strong follow-through in shotgunning. This is true in everything—but vitally important if you want to score well on doves.

The fine shot literally "drives" his gun barrel past the target, shoots, and keeps swinging. One of the advantages of this is that when you do miss, if you continue to follow through you'll be very likely to see why you missed; whether you shot over the bird or behind or whatever. This is the secret of the man who is so deadly with the second shot—he misses, sees why, corrects his swing, and picks up the bird with his backup shell. That's another reason to pick out one bird and stay with it—not miss one, then turn and fire at another bird and likely miss that one as well. A good method of practice is to shoot a few clay targets and pick the big piece and break that one with a second shot after you've broken the bird with the first. A couple of dollars invested in a handtrap and a case of targets is money well spent.

I like to shoot partners, taking turns shooting and marking the downed birds for each other. The great trick here is to pick the ideal buddy. Ideally he shoots the same gauge gun you do so you can bum shells, and in the evening gin-rummy game he has enough sense to knock the first chance he gets. His memory should be selective—having total recall on just how you made those sensational shots and dimming out on the times you missed birds you could have hit with your shoe. If you travel together it is vital that he does not snore like a chain saw, and that he gets up at least 15 minutes before you do, letting you sleep while he dresses and shaves. It goes without saying that he doesn't mind plucking your birds as well as his, and he puts the extra bird in your pile in case of an odd number.

In states where morning shooting is permitted, I don't know of many things I enjoy more than a predawn breakfast of biscuits, ham, grits, and red-eye gravy with my dove-hunting buddies the morning of opening day. The chitchat about the ultimate new gun, the secret solutions to doing better than 50-50, and the very candid evaluations of everyone else's ability. (This is where I learned, the hard way, the truth found in the old adage about bragging after the shoot, not before.)

In the pink of early dawn the dove field is held in the silence of promise. The shooters shuffle around making practice swings against the last light from the morning star. A silent wish or so forms in my mind as my partner and I stand ready—and for the last time that morning I have my 8s in the pocket they belong in and the 7½s in their proper place.

From far away we can hear the murmuring of the early flocks and before we are really aware of their coming, doves in twos and threes and fours appear as if born from the morning mists, and the soft coughs of distant shotguns tells us this will be a day of days.

Dove season, to the man who loves the mysteries of the shotgun, is the beginning of his year. In the little lulls between the flights, his mind wanders ahead to October woodcock and November quail and ducks. He takes a tough quartering dove and smiles to himself as he marks the fall. Aglow with the certain knowledge that he has made a shot that few men can repeat, he pats his shotgun with as much affection as he would show a favorite dog. There's a magic thing between us two, he thinks almost half-aloud, and begins that short-lived dream of a man who would be a shooting legend to his friends.

But let's leave him there, as we would sometimes walk quietly from our very selves, enmeshed in dreams of doves with every shot. Let him have his minute—it will not last. For we know that no matter how steady the hand or sharp the eye and how perfect the gun, no man was ever born to be as good as 50-50 shooting doves in front of all his friends.

BIG SPENDERS

I sent a letter off recently that contained two $1 bills, covering an order for two heavy bass leaders. Then I stopped to figure out why. First off, I don't need any fly rod leaders for bass. I've got a dozen or more. Second, tying my own leaders is one of the few things I know how to do—and therefore I enjoy doing it. Third, I don't really need to get mail. I already get too many catalogs, bills, and assorted pleadings for my concern, interest, and charity, plus the usual assortment of alluring real estate offers and other similar investments.

Why then the leaders? I'll give you an answer as honest as sweat. I just like buying something, and that's about all the money I had loose that I could throw away.

Remember all the stuff like that you used to be able to buy for a nickel or a dime or even pennies? A cheap magnifying glass. Split rings that would hold a flashlight or a set of keys. Whistles. A half-pack of Old Golds. A sack of Bull Durham. A corncob pipe. All that stuff from the Five and Ten when they only charged 5 cents and 10 cents. Not to mention the glorious array of candy, soda, cookies, and other tooth-rotting delights: licorice whips, candy whistles, packages of caramel-covered stuff that also contained some kind of toy. I know that few things are more boring to my children than a recitation involving finances and the good old days, but they don't understand that it wasn't so much that you wanted the product, as it was that you just wanted to *buy* something; something that you really didn't need, but a luxury. Something that you weren't afraid of wearing out or losing. You just wanted to go up to the counter, tap the glass with your Indian head nickel, and indulge a fleeting whim with hard cash.

Note that I didn't include any of the mass of fishing stuff you could buy for a dime or so. Or flashlight batteries, or leather shoelaces, or boxes of .22s. Those were necessities; serious and planned purchases for purely functional reasons.

I guess I was, and must admit I still am, a junk buyer. Not essentially pure junk, but stuff I don't need, or already have in life-time-supply numbers. Pliers, for instance. I'm a pliers freak. I still have the set that came in our old Model A Ford. I have a set that belonged to my grandfather. I have a set in all the cars, in all my fishing tackle boxes, in my vests, in my gun stuff boxes. And a few sets just lying around. Same with screwdrivers; maybe worse.

My buying pliers is akin to an illiterate who stocks up on encyclopedias. They look good lying around but he has no real ability to use them. My gunsmith shudders when he sees me with a new set of screwdrivers, knowing that for the next month he'll be busy replacing ruined screws in my guns. The only thing I can do well with a hammer is crack hickory nuts. But show me a cheap and guaranteed shoddy set of tools, preferably in a fitted plastic case that I can throw in with my outdoor gear, and I've got my hand in my pocket as fast as a striking snake.

There just isn't a lot of stuff around anymore that a guy can afford to say "What the hell" and grab, so what there is of it you tend to stock up. Tubes of glue. Nobody ever has enough glue. Odd scraps in a leather shop. Never know when you'll need a little

piece of leather. If you've got leather and glue you can spend a
whole rainy day covering recoil pads or pasting bottoms on ash-
trays. How about bottles of stuff to refinish stocks. Got to have a lot
of that, right? Did you ever finish a stock that looked anywhere near
half-decent? No. And neither have I. I was bumming around
George Schielke's gun shop the other day, debating whether to buy
my 500th red handkerchief (60 cents) or my 50th pair of red suspenders ($1.50), when I spotted a new kind of stock refinisher ($1).
I asked George if it was any good. "Not especially," George said,
"but I like to sell it because I can get it off the stock easy after
you're through fooling around with it."

There's a lot to be said for something you can buy, fool around
with, and still do little enough damage so someone else can undo
what you did and do it over right.

Back in the days when I did a fair amount of shooting, I used
to carry an overnight bag filled with useful, useless stuff. A can of
moleskin to raise and lower the height of comb on my trapstock.
Plastic shims and spacers to adjust the pitch of the stock and alter
the length of pull. Instant blue. Yellow chalk for the rib in bad light.
Spare trigger parts that I had no idea how to install. Ditto firing
pins. Ditto front beads. And lord only knows what else—not counting screwdrivers and pliers. And, do you know, I don't believe I
ever used one single, solitary thing out of that bag. But nothing
could ever have persuaded me to leave it home. A dedicated trapshooter has to carry so many pounds of gear and accessories—not
counting spare guns, extra barrels, shells, shooting glasses, rain
gear, gloves, bug repellent, and/or whiskey, depending on the time
of the year and the area.

My hunting bag wasn't a gram lighter, but contained a different variety of stuff. Not any more utilitarian, but different. English
shell extractors, cleaning rods, extra whistles, flashlight (just imagine how well it worked if you ever needed it!), adhesive bandages,
tweezers, extra collars and leashes, odds and ends of various shells,
screwdrivers and pliers. Never anything so down-to-earth as pipe
cleaners, a dry pair of socks, or a clean handkerchief.

Both bags were stolen from my car a couple of years ago, and
I've never bothered to really replace them completely. I still carry

about 50 percent of the same items, but have them haphazardly strewn around my coat pockets, where they stay until the annual cleaning out and emerge a sort of strange brown color from being marinated in bits of pipe and chewing tobacco and weed seeds.

The pattern is still there: Call it a $2 syndrome if you like, because that's about what it really is. I guess I'll always buy just about anything remotely connected with hunting and shooting for $1.98. Maybe more than one. I guess I'd feel guilty (guiltier?) about spending any more. But not as guilty as if I spent as much time as I do hanging around the kind of places I hang around and not buying anything.

Buying something gives you a sense of self-respect. It deludes the proprietor (maybe) into thinking "Today a pair of suspenders . . . tomorrow a Midas Grade Browning." But more importantly, it deludes us into thinking exactly the same thing.

A famous theatre producer, Charles McArthur, once offered the great Helen Hayes a dish of peanuts at a party and said to her, "I wish they were emeralds."

So it is with us and our 50-cent red bandannas, our $1 stock restorer, and our 89-cent pliers. We are saying, in effect, to the gentleman behind the counter, "I wish it was $500," and he, with a smile, as he hands us our little brown paper bag, is saying "I wish it was a Midas Grade."

HITS AND MS.

There seems to be quite a movement on to avoid mentioning the gender of people, places, and things—lest one or the other gender take offense.

We now have chairpersons, repairpersons, firepersons and so on. We'll have to say, "Who was that person I saw you with last night?" "That was no person, that was my spouse."

I even understand that one of my favorite chickens, the Rhode Island Red, has undergone, or is undergoing, a name change to avoid the taint of possible Communist leanings. Seriously, they really are, and I think that's ridiculous. All the Rhode Island Reds I've ever known were strong individualists—the kind of chickens that would vote a straight Republican ticket.

I'm a little uneasy with all this fooling around with the English language. They're going to end up messing around with buck and doe, hen and rooster, drakes and ducks, and fox and vixen and so on until nobody knows what anybody is talking about.

I'm all for Women's Liberation. In fact I take pride in being one of the early proponents. My wife has always had her own shovel, her own hammer and saw, her own paintbrushes, and even her own ax. I've always let her do her share of the chores so she'll feel equal. If I shovel snow off the walk, I'm meticulous not to do more than half. When we reshingled the garage roof, I only did one side and let her pleasure herself with the other. All I ask is that she doesn't insist we call each other some kind of "person." Or have herself addressed as Ms. That form of salutation seems to always strike my eye as something that's been misspelled.

As far as I'm concerned, women can be my equal all they want. I'm delighted that my daughters like to fish and shoot. They can grow up and do and be anything they please. But I want them to be proud of being ladies, not persons. And I don't want them fiddling around with confusing designations. I have a hard enough time with the language as it is now.

It took me a long time to recognize a hen trout from the male, and now they're trying to take that away from me. What fun is there in trying to remember that a male swan is called a cob, if I risk offending some person's ears? What's going to happen to outdoor writers if they can't, every so often, refer to "Old Betsy"?

I enjoy, in an emergency, a modest and sparing touch of profanity. It's part of our language that's colorful, imaginative, and lends itself to individual touches. I'm right there with Mark Twain, who reminds us that "in certain circumstances, urgent circumstances, desperate circumstances, profanity furnishes a relief denied even to prayer." If I happen to shoot way behind an easy crossing shot, as occasionally happens, a quiet "son-of-a-person" isn't going to give me the relief I need.

Can you say "fisherperson" out loud without feeling silly? "Fisherwoman" sounds slighting and apologetic. "Angler" always creates an image with me of someone who won't stoop to using anything but a No. 20 dry fly and a bamboo rod. I guess I'm always going to call ladies that fish, fishermen, and start catching hell for it. A man can't even say he's in the doghouse without risking the stripe of male chauvinism. I don't know what the neuter of that would be except canine, and even the lady lawyers I know wouldn't go that far. What about "sportsman," "sportswoman," and "sportsperson"?

I know what sounds good to my not-really-arrogant ear. I know what I'm going to go on saying; I just hope they're really liberal about it.

I also trust that women will give this whole designation thing a lot of thought before they pass a bunch of laws or something about who's supposed to be called what. It's hard enough today to figure out what flag a lot of young people are flying under, and if they refuse to be titled Miss or Mr. it's going to cause a lot of unnecessary embarrassment.

I must admit I didn't like it when it became faddish for public places to get cute with the designation of their restrooms. You know what I mean: squaws and braves, bucks and does, sort of thing. But what if the genderless craze goes any further? Will they end up with symbols? I've seen that tried and can report with some embarrassment that it doesn't always work: top hats and high heels or skirts and trousers aren't that quick a demarcation when you're in a bit of a hurry in a dark hallway. I'll stand with "Ladies" and "Gentlemen." Crude, maybe, but surefire.

I know some men lavish more attention on their dogs than they do on their wives. And that's just not fair. Dogs can't cook or do laundry or mending. And I'd be willing to bet anything that there are more good wives around than top-flight dogs anyway. But what if (and I know it's absolutely impossible in these trying times) a young husband could send his wife out to be trained? Few young men are capable of doing the job themselves, because like a man with his first bird dog, he's really not sure what to expect her to do. He's not ready to make a decision about whether to be firm or permissive. He's probably not sure what he really wants himself.

A man picking a puppy from a litter faces the same problems as a man choosing a wife. He looks at the mother and gets a pretty good idea of what the future companion will act like. But now he's torn between good looks and function. He knows how hard it is to get both in the same package—but with an innocence that brings tears to my eyes, he opts for good looks and hopes that he'll be the one in a million that got lucky. Now he might be just that. And then again he might not.

But if he got one that was trained, he can see what can be done and decide if that's what he really wants. In the old days, before my time, daughters were trained at home and the family showed them off like the jewels they were. Suitors were invited over for supper and the girl's family constantly reminded the young gentlemen that although the beaten biscuits were incredibly light, and the pie was ambrosia and would lock in First Place in all tests from flavor to digestability, that Susan was capable of even more culinary genius. Embroidery was exhibited. The fact that she made all her own clothes was disclosed. She could churn butter, make soap, and was handy at hog-butchering time. She was famous in her church group for being obedient, kind, and thrifty, and always spoke in a soft, quiet voice. She could bake bread, cobble shoes, and her grape jelly won prizes in fairs. She was a one-person industry and came equipped with a dowry. Ah, those were the days!

I've toyed with the idea of writing a book on the subject of such training. But who would buy it? A swain handing one to his fiancée would place himself in three kinds of peril, and women would march in protest or worse in front of the stores that handled it. Maybe a book on training a young lout to be a good husband would go better. Maybe best I stay out of it altogether. I don't make as many decisions around my own house as I'd like you to believe, anyway.

Maybe this will all turn out alright in the long run. Most women I know are as smart as their husbands, as hard-working or more so, and 100 percent of them are nicer looking and smell better. Men have been doing what women tell them to do since Eve offered Adam the apple, but there's been a truce that lets this go on without talking about it. And now women want to bring it out in the open—and fool around with our vocabulary and spelling in the bargain. But I for one hope it's just a fad, like the raising or lowering of a hemline, or shooting trap with improved-cylinder barrels.

Maybe I ought to write my congressperson. But on second thought, there's always the chance that fisherpersons will start baiting my hook for me and letting me in the boat first and lighting my pipe. Maybe I'll play the helpless male and see what happens. Then, maybe I'd better not.

Ms. Hill would raise hl.

ONLY

I remember a long time ago when I lost a setter puppy who fell through the spring ice on my pond. The grief I felt was probably out of proportion, considering all the other tragedies a man has to cope with, but I was for several days deeply morose and heartsick. During this time a friend called me up to go fishing. I refused, told him that I wasn't in the mood, and why. And I've never really forgiven him for saying, "It was only a dog."

There are some things, animate and inanimate, that I hold so dear that to even imagine anyone saying "It's only an old fly rod" or "It's only a worn-out knife" can fill me with coldness, anger, or regret.

Be it admitted that I hold on too hard to some memories and common things that go along with them—but there it is.

I like to recall, when I am waxing my thread-bandaged salmon rod, the days when I could truly say I have never been happier.

An old shotgun, no longer much used but kept around for cleaning purposes, brings back a younger me, an assortment of bird dogs that only their owner would remember with a smile, and a few friends I can now hunt with in memory alone.

That's part of the magic of "things." They can by their simple presence create a childish anticipation or recall a moment that, without them, would be dimmed or lost. And far from having too many, I can recall with regret a too-long list of things I wish I had had the sense to save.

I'd like to know whatever happened to my old Stevens .22 that was the major tool of my farm-boy trapline years. Or a bamboo bait-casting rod that was once my pride and joy. Where did all the tinted picture postcards go that showed my 20-year-old father with an 8-pound largemouth bass? My spring-run sucker spear made from grandpa's old circle saw? No doubt they were picked up somewhere by someone who held them briefly in his hand and only saw some damaged, rusted, faded, or unknown thing, and said "only an old postcard" or "only junk." And so, no doubt, it was to him, and, having no old friend to speak for it, it disappeared.

I'm sure, as well, that someone misses the old Vomhofe reel I picked up for a song just to have this "thing" that I know was used to fish the Restigouche or some such salmon river and had seen the kind of days that I'll never have a chance to know. I've got a few other things that sort of introduce me to an unknown man or a different time that I would have liked to share.

Decoys that kissed the Chesapeake when limits were dictated only by conscience and the amount of money you could afford for shells.

An inexpensive unnamed hammer-double, hand-polished white a touch ahead of where the splinter forend ends. I pick it up and put my hand right there and swing it now and then and try to listen to the cans and redheads and pintails as they whistled by in flocks that I can picture stretching for several hundred yards across the wild celery flats.

A gunning light—an oil lamp set in a wooden box that once held shells and a piece of broken mirror glued behind it. Think of the nights this had been sculled across the water to enchant a flock of swans or geese or ducks that had a fancy New York or Baltimore restaurant as their next port-of-call . . . to swim their last in brandied gravy.

Things past. Things future: an unfished fly rod that I intend to baptize in some very special place that will announce itself to me at just the proper time. A three-inch side-by-side picked up too late last year to use for geese, already showing just a bit of wear from being handled—just to get the feel. And a couple of other odds and ends that I foresee sharing good days to come for many, many years. A pup that will by fall, I hope, start my gunning season with a perfect long retrieve. Depending, of course, on who ends up training whom!

The function of these things is as often secret and personal as it is obvious. To pick up something for tomorrow is a pleasant way to pretend that tomorrow will not find you somewhat older. A new puppy to work with is the perfect hedge against time. A new shotgun or fishing rod is, for the likes of us, a near-guarantee of a dramatic increase in our shooting skills and our casting technique. Just as saving the old stuff can serve to remind us of what we once were—strong, tireless, and living in a world that was for a time constantly new and better.

It's funny that so many things that are "only this or that" to the other world (where they put their savings in the bank and give their old stuff to charity) are to us a savings of a sort and a charity that we believe in—deeply.

I like to think that my old stuff will grow in interest and that someone, someday, will be delighted that I saved it just for them— whoever they may turn out to be.

The little things I keep around that some call "onlys" tell me for sure that there was a Little Ben, that there were great runs of salmon, and ghosts called canvasback and sprig. Which is important, for I'm afraid that we might someday become a country where the people that we trust right now will say, before passing on to more important things, "Only ducks, only fish, and who needs a bird dog anymore?"

So I keep my little bank account of things, knowing that the less important they seem to more and more people, the more important they will seem to me and those who I hope will someday care.

I can think of lots of "onlys" that I'd like to see again, some frivolous, some not. Only a field without a NO HUNTING sign. Only a six-point elk. Only another Parker. Only a kid trapping muskrats for school money. Only a dollar box of 12-gauge shells. Only a handmade swan decoy. Only a flock of plover.

Well, they all can't say "If only somebody cared." Because a lot of us do, even if we're "only hunters and fishermen."

CHORES

I was born a slave to a monster. It was a big, six-lid wood stove with a hood and a warming oven on the top and a huge oven that could easily handle a 25-pound turkey and a pie or so on the bottom. On one side was a well for hot water. There was a big chair pulled up next to this, and it was everybody's favorite seat. I never got to sit there much unless no one else was home.

When you cooked and heated the kitchen with a wood stove you became very particular about firewood and kindling. Especially if it was your job to keep it going and make sure it was started in the morning.

We favored chestnut for kindling. It was plentiful, thanks to the blight that left our woods full of dead and seasoned wood, and it split like a dream. We'd cut cord after pungent cord and rick it in the barn—the grown men did that. Thereafter it was up to me to make the adjustment from log into inch-square kindling—normally the kind of work a kid enjoys. He's got a small ax of his own, a whetstone, and a big sharpening wheel that you pedal while you sit on an old tractor seat attached to the grindstone's frame.

But winter used to set in pretty early, and after the first flush of pride and fiddling with the grindstone the bloom quickly faded from the rose. I'd split a big basketful, stack it neatly in the kitchen woodbox, and almost before I could turn around, it seemed, it had disappeared. About November the routine became a choice of splitting kindling at night before I went to bed, or getting up a half-hour early and splitting it then. Whoever coined the phrase "a choice of two evils" might very well have been in much the same dilemma.

Then, on top of the kindling problem, there was the woodbox itself. Forever empty or nearly so, no matter how avidly one piled wood precariously up over the top. About the only thrill you got from carrying wood was the odd time when a mouse, still in some deep midwinter sleep, suddenly awoke to find himself transported on the wood in your arms and made a wild dash up across a shoulder and around the back of your neck. Whereupon you searched thoroughly to make sure he wasn't down inside your shirt, picked up the armload you'd dropped, and spent the next few trips inspecting every stick until the incident was forgotten, and about that time it happened all over again.

In those days you went to school with eagerness. The few chores the teacher placed on you were considered an honor and a sign of responsibility—they had a flavor and character different from chores at home, no matter the similarity. One of my school jobs, first thing in the morning, was to walk to the neighboring farm (my grandfather's—which meant that more often than not my grandmother would be waiting for me with a couple of freshly baked cookies) to fetch water. The well was a sweet-smelling, moss-lined lattice house, and the water was retrieved with an old wooden windlass that was about an inch or two too far back for me to reach in for the pail and swing it out to pour without getting about a quarter of it all over my pants and shoes. Responsibility is always exacted and proven at some personal cost.

My other daily chore—since the one-room school was also

heated with a big stove—was chopping and fetching kindling. If they ever gave out grades for splitting chestnut, I'd have gotten an A+. After all, if you do something with that regularity for eight years, something has to happen. It might have been the only A+ I got in school, too, but I forget. Being a dreamer, I suspect I might have done pretty well in geography.

Kids then, and a lot of the girls included, thought nothing of having their own hatchet, knife, and a gun when the legal time came—maybe even a little early if you were way out in the country on the farm. They were all considered tools. Things to be used, to be careful of, to take care of—and in doing so increase the pleasure of their function. "A sharp ax is not half as dangerous as a dull one," is a remark I must have heard a thousand times when my father or grandfather passed an appraising thumb over the blade I was using.

Your ax or hatchet was yours—alone. It seems to me that it was an unspoken law that under no circumstances did anyone ever ask to borrow your ax or pocketknife. I know that guns were asked for and freely loaned, but cutting tools—never.

When you were entrusted with an ax you knew that the next symbol of being grown up and considered trustworthy was having your own gun—or at least being allowed to use one of those scattered around the house. (The .22 was usually kept in the barn so it was handy for red squirrels, crows, and snakes. The shotguns were in the kitchen closet leaning against a shelf that held various boxes of Xpert, Ranger, Nitro Express, and Peters High Velocity.)

My first .22 was parallel in time with running a small in-the-morning-before-school trapline. It was used to dispatch skunks, which are the pungent bread and butter of the novitiate. The rifle was a single-shot, falling-block Stevens, completely useless at distances over ten feet as far as any accuracy was concerned—which, as I think about it, is probably why someone gave it to me. It also rarely ejected a shell, which meant that part of my clanging set of trapping tools included a pair of cheap pliers.

My trapping money, in 35-cent increments for a possum and around $2 per skunk, gradually swelled to around $7 or $8, which graduated me to a single-shot, bolt-action Winchester .22. I really wanted one of the pump-action, tubular-magazine jobs, but wiser heads who knew my temperament and the price of ammunition rightly figured that shortly I'd be borrowing ammunition money against nonexistent fur futures. Somehow they knew that if I had a rifle that held 18 shells, I'd use up every one every time I loaded the rifle. They never admitted they would have done the same thing, but I think that's how they knew I would.

When the trapping season was over the year I was eligible for my first hunting license—I had to be 11—I had somehow frittered away my money on various odds and ends and maybe a necessity or two like hip boots and a new flashlight. My summer job money, 50 cents a day rowing boats for the summer bass fisherman on the lake, was spent for fishing tackle as fast as I earned it. And as hunting season neared, the $10 I needed for a long-selected, single-shot 20-gauge might as well have been $10,000.

I had to have some kind of a job—of which there weren't any in the first place, and in the second place there wasn't much I could do that was worth money. Except one thing: chopping kindling. There was a job that most men considered a nuisance, that consumed time better put to other uses, and the ladies were glad to avoid the splinters and wood mice, given half a chance.

So it all worked out. Kindling provided the gun and a couple of boxes of shells, tiding me over until cold weather brought on the trapping season.

Years later, when I was in college, I sat listening to a very famous professor of American history lecture on how skill with the ax was one of the primary reasons that the early settlers were able to begin the westward movement—clearing land for small farms, living on them for a year or two, and moving on.

As I listened I sat up straight and proud, sharing secretly the sure knowledge that had I been a pioneer, my ax and I would have seen us through. After all, I'd been there myself, in my own small way, many years before.

MAKE A WISH

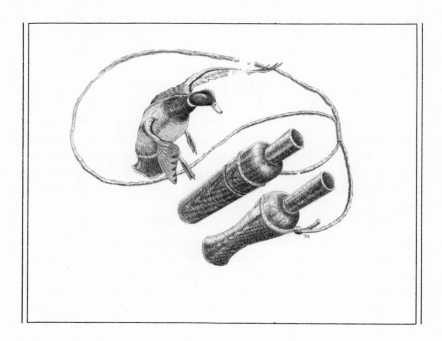

Nowhere is it writ, as far as I know, that wishing for something you will probably never have—or that is impossible—is against the law. A wish is a conscious dream.

That's one of the nicer things about Christmastime; we're encouraged to let our wishes fly—both aloud, written, and, more often, in secret. (I think a Christmas wish that we know will never come true is a lot closer to life than a New Year's Eve promise we know we'll never keep!)

Now, you know you've got to be careful about what you wish for—because wishes have an unpredictable way of coming true. We all know of the kind of old fables where someone was granted three wishes, and the third wish was to undo the first two.

I remember wishing, when I was several generations younger, that I had some help in carrying in wood. Then I got a little brother. Now, whoever it was that granted that answer to that wish might have been right in theory, but he didn't have too sharp an eye on the practical side of things.

Another example: A friend of mine who kept badgering his wife to go hunting with him; she kept saying that as much as she liked the idea, she was just *positive* she'd never learn to hit anything with a shotgun. So, as sort of a "Why not give it a try" gesture he sent her to the Orvis shooting school, and now she's at least even money to bag half again as many birds as he does.

I'll bet you wish you had some of the old guns that you traded off because you wished you had something different at the time. I know I can count at least five. Yessir, you go around wishing out loud in the wrong place at the wrong time, and you're going to end up wishing you hadn't.

You take a guy who has never been salmon fishing and you wish him the best of luck. Then you spend all fall wishing he'd finally quit telling everybody how many he caught, and how many *you* caught. (For salmon fishing, feel very free to substitute deer hunting, goose shooting, trap, skeet, elk, or whatever comeuppance you're most recently familiar with.)

I'd gamble, however, with throwing up a couple of kid-type wishes just to see how I'd make out, because no matter what happened, I don't see, right now, how I'd end up worse off. I wish I could ride a horse. Now, that might not sound like a real wish as opposed to the avoidance of working a little at something, but it is. I have worked at riding, but somehow the parts of the puzzle don't fit comfortably together. Real-life cowboys have said, "Son, you look real good up there." Look real good I may, but the horse knows and I know that looking good isn't the part that counts. I'd trade a lot of looking-good charm for a little feeling-good comfort.

I wish I could shoot "just one bird at a time" at trap instead of constantly puzzling over the one I just missed or the bad angle I know will show up the next time I call "Pull."

I wish I could quit acting like I was 11 years old every time I get involved in a covey of quail, a flock of ducks, or a double-rise on grouse and woodcock. Lord knows I know better than to cut away at the whole bunch instead of picking out just one bird at a time—

but the Lord also knows a lot of other things I do that I ought to know better.

I wish I could remember not to forget things. I've got rain gear, pipes, flashlights, hats, socks, pocketknives, alarm clocks, and other assorted items scattered around camps in most of the United States and several other countries. Maybe it's because I always feel so pleased with myself that I remember to bring that sort of thing that it proves my "other wish" theory is really working. But by now I'm sort of resigned to being whatever it is that I am—living proof that the old saying "If wishes were horses, beggars would ride" has a lot going for it.

But on the other hand, there are always some close external objects, like wives who now and then have wishes that run contrary to or at least a little aslant of ours. At one time, when I wished I'd smoke less, I began chewing tobacco more. My wife began wishing, very vocally, that I chew less—or at least less when I was at the Ladies Gun Club picnic or other similar high-society functions. It's just a fact of life that some people's wishes come true easier and quicker than others. Especially if the other people are married to you and you rely on them for roasting your geese, patching your gunning clothes, and remembering to pack your long underwear.

I've quit wishing that I was a really better shot, a nifty fly-caster, or a reasonably intelligent poker player; I've discovered that I've got a lot in common with a lot of nice people the way I am, and I hear that it's lonely at the top—I'll never know, but that's what I hear.

I've thought a lot about it lately, and if I could have one small and simple wish to hand out as a Christmas present to those who need it, it would be that all those small boys and girls who get a new gun or fishing rod could step right outside and use it. I never got a new fishing rod for Christmas, but I did get a gun once and had the ultimate satisfaction of being able to step out into the kitchen garden and run a couple of shells through it and feel the immense pleasure from that little bite of recoil and the drifting smell of powder—both a lot more meaningful when the gun is yours and yours alone. I think I'll take back that part about "small boys and girls." Whoever it is, you or me or Luanne or little Howard, let's grab all we can of something being new and ours. If there's something wrong with a grownup standing in the snow in slippers throwing a plug or a fly up the driveway or highballing at some imaginary mallard flock with a brand-new call, I fail to see it. If you get a down-filled hunting coat, I hope it's below zero so you can try it out. If you get new boots, I wish you a puddle two feet deep by the kitchen door! And finally, I wish that whoever hears your wishes smiles on you with understanding every now and then.

DON'T STOP ME
IF YOU'VE HEARD THIS ONE

In Britain, where a man considers his family to be slightly second-ary to his dog and hunting and fishing activities, the Great Debate still goes on: Does a woodcock actually carry her young in flight? Among those who say "yes" there is a secondary question: Does she carry them on her back or between her tiny thighs? Mind you, that in this day and age of incredible photographic feats none of this has ever been documented—cash prizes offered notwithstanding. Gentlemen who have served together in blooded regiments have been known to stop speaking to each other over their convictions pro or con. Letters to sporting magazines about seeing this mater-nal feat are in ready supply. But, as we noted, no pictures.

I, for one, would like to believe that a woodcock can and does carry her young—tiny walnut-sized fluffs of down—tucked se-curely between her legs. But the weights-and-measures side of me is still skeptical.

So it is with a lot of outdoor lore; we would like to believe, or indeed strongly hold, that certain rather improbable things are indeed true. We *want* to believe because it helps keep the mystery alive. It keeps man from becoming all-knowing and too powerful.

I grew up, as I'm sure a lot of us did, believing that a horsehair if put into the water would turn into an eel. I also believed that if you killed a snake you had to be alert for the mate seeking revenge. I'm not sure I believed that a cat had nine lives—but it's possible.

Hunters' tales have always tended to the unusual, the bizarre, and the unlikely. Not what I would call lies exactly, but colorful exaggerations. A woodcock carrying her young or a fox running backward to fool the dogs may be capable of raising an eyebrow or starting a skeptical smile, but imagine the courage of our forefathers who brought back vivid stories of centaurs, unicorns, flame-breathing dragons, and a vast assortment of serpents capable of awesome feats. I'm not sure what all the ancient versions of "bourbon and branch" were, but they must have been equally awesome to have inspired some of the stories—and to have kept the wanderer's audience nodding in concurrence.

I'm still impressed by the feats of bravery it must have taken in those long-ago days to set sail on uncharted seas, or blaze a trail through what the old maps used to label "Terra Incognita." I'm still impressed with the kind of devil-may-care curiosity that induced some starving (I'm sure this had to be a factor) soul to eat the first oyster or clam. That's a lot of adventure right there, as anyone who's tried to lure a skeptical four-year-old to try collards or squash will quickly agree.

I think we're all intrigued by what might just possibly be true. I know a lot of old farmers who believed implicitly in the hoop snake—the one that put its tail into its mouth and rolled away like a hoop. And the glass snake—which, when struck, shattered to pieces.

I'll bet that, right today, there is an old-timer or two around who will tell you, in deep sincerity, stories about eagles carrying away a human baby. And there have been so many stories about wolves caring for human foundlings that someone still around will have known of this from "personal experience."

I don't remember who it was that said, "I don't believe anything I hear and only half what I see." But he couldn't have been a gunner or fisherman—most of whom hold with the exact reverse. I'm a little bit of a skeptic myself at times, but probably out of a little jealousy because the most interesting things always seem to involve someone else. Like my onetime neighbor who had a wild grouse that would come out of the woods and follow him around whenever he started his lawn mower. I'd give a lot if that was my story in the original. (Maybe someday it'll turn out that way . . .) It's the kind of story I like—even though it ruined Harold's fall hunting in one of his favorite covers.

I also like stories about a bird dog that comes and finds his owner and leads him back to where the dog has been on point. Or the one I've saved from an old newspaper (you've got to believe what's in print—right?) about a bird dog that fell into an abandoned well when he was bringing back a dead quail and still had it in his mouth when he was rescued two days later.

No sir, those marvelous stories that others can drink on and are constantly pleaded with to tell and retell, never happen right here. Of course, I've had a couple of strange things happen on fishing trips, but the minute I mention them someone interrupts and tops the one I had in mind, or the room empties and men who haven't been near a sink in years find an excuse to do the camp dishes, leaving my incredible ending to be heard only by a drowsy retriever.

But I'm ready. As they say, where there's smoke there's fire. And next time a woodcock flushes in front of me on one of my midsummer evening walks, I'll be looking for a tiny passenger tucked up there in the first-class section. But that'll be the easy part. What's hard is finding someone to tell it to—but maybe with the room full of the magic smoke from an applewood fire and just the right amount of a well-known by-product of corn, I'll find a descendant of a man who was persuasive when he told about seeing a unicorn, or an eagle carrying a baby.

SIXES AND SEVENS

We all know what shot is—those little round lead pellets that come in two sizes, the size you need and the size you probably have with you.

Having the right size shot is as rare as having the right kind of fly—rarer, really, because 25 shotshells weigh a little more and take up more room than 25 Olive Duns. What happens is that we've all read the charts put out by the ammunition companies and, trusting dreamers that we are, we believe them. Now that's fair, provided you believe them in the calm air of the hardware store or the gun-shop, because they work there. Where they don't work like that is in a duck marsh, for example.

Let's say you've read X number of articles by the wise sages who speak from experience well exhibited by their wind-creased smiles that circle gnarled brier pipes. The Sage talks knowingly of

No. 6 shot being the cat's pajamas for decoying broadbills. You put your magazine down and ask your wife, as soon as she finishes patching your hippers, not to forget that you want a couple boxes of 6s out of her reloader. About 3¼-1¼ should be fine.

"No 4s?" she asks.

"No 4s," you tell her patiently, "I've just finished a piece by a guy who knows all there is to know about shot sizes, and he's convinced me." You continue, as she puts another log on the fire and freshens your drink, "I'm sure he's right. You remember last year when I told you about missing those ducks—easy crossing shots they were too, off Cedar Island—well I had 4s then. Too open a pattern; 6s would have done the job."

Saturday morning finds you in a blind facing 40 lovely bluebill decoys, placed in a classic hook layout. Perfect, right? Wrong! Oh, there are plenty of birds alright, but they're out there about 54 yards. Just exactly where 6s quit and good heavy 4s are just the ticket. But we all know where the 4s are—sitting in neat rows over your wife's reloading bench.

Actually the problem isn't as impossible as it used to be. It's still difficult, but things are looking up. The late Cliff Baldwin, who once worked as a road man for Remington, told me that he had to carry (this is back in the 20s) BBs, 2s, 3s, 4s, 5s, 6s, 7s, 8s, 9s, 10s, and 12s. Both in drop and chilled shot for the most part. And in various dram equivalents. And in 8 gauge, 10 gauge, 12 gauge, 14 gauge, 16 gauge, 20 gauge, 24 gauge, 28 gauge, .410s and—for the true small-bore gentlemen—32 gauge.

You wanted a 2-dram, 1-ounce load of 8s for your 12-gauge woodcock gun? No problem. How about 2 ounces of No. 3 in copper shot in your 10 gauge? Right! Just the ticket for 60-yard Canadas.

And you couldn't stump Cliff with your own ideas on what might be the money load for a live-bird shoot at the old Chalfont traps. If you decided that 3½ drams of No. 7 copper shot were what you wanted for the choke barrel and 3¼ drams of 8½s were an absolute necessity for the first shot—why, there were plenty of ammunition companies ready and willing to turn out a few cases for you—if your shooting ability was a respectable advertisement.

Shot and loads weren't the only consideration, either, that kept many an old gunner muttering to himself and his Lucky Strike bred pointer. There were plenty who wouldn't bet a good chew on their chances if they didn't have Laflin & Rand powder. And plenty of others who wouldn't pull a trigger unless it set off a good charge of Audubon or Du Pont or Robinhood or Hazard's Ducking No. 1.

Yessir, those were the good old days. When a man could start a fight or bet a Connecticut-built Derby hat about the qualities of greased felt wads, cardboard wads, hair wads, cork or linen wads—their combination, number, size, and the order they were placed in the shell.

I figure that a man with a Grade A Parker who set out to buy a season's worth of partridge loads just didn't walk into the feed store and ask for a box of light 7s. That wouldn't have any style. He wouldn't have felt right about it.

He would have spent some time over a Mason jar of home-made apple and discussed the whole thing with his shell man. Where was he going to hunt the whole months of October and November? How were his Llewellin setters working out? Did it look like a late fall or an early one? Plenty of young birds or a scattering of old wise ones? A variety of odds and ends were weighed and measured, the order placed, and in due time handsome and colorful wooden cartons filled with shells packed in boxes adorned with the work of a fine artist arrived. They hefted right, and the long polished brass bases gleamed with efficiency. And all that season, after each shot, he carefully blew out the remaining heavy smoke from each barrel and inhaled the pungent perfume with deep satisfaction, before sending the dogs for his fallen partridge.

Now I know, I suppose, that the shells I can buy at the filling station are fine, but somehow I miss the serious give-and-take of the old days. And suppose I want 7s or 3s. I can't have them. I've got to settle for 8s or 7½s or 8½s or 9s or 2s or 4s. But I've got one advantage over the gentleman with the Grade A. I have to make do with what's around—and he didn't. We can come home drooling marsh ooze on the floor and console ourselves with beaten home-made biscuits and a long discussion with the Better Half on how different things might have been if the grocery store had carried the 5s we wanted instead of having had to make do with 4s or 6s.

Just as there is no perfect shotgun, except somebody else's, the perfect shot size is most likely to be the one we don't have with us—just as we rarely have the right choke for the job at hand.

I'm sure somewhere it must be written that when I go ducking with my full choke and heavy 4s I will have no shots over 22 yards. And no need to get a headache guessing what happens when I'm ready, improved and modified, with a coat full of 7½s.

I have come to believe that if the biblical Job lived close to fine woodcock cover, the day he chose 9s, he wouldn't get one flush under 40 yards.

One thing for sure, there's no right answer. And that's what is so much fun. Somehow I seem to sleep better in a gunning camp when the last words I hear, before dreaming of a perfect double on quail, are about drop shot versus chilled and light 8s versus three drams of 9s.

CLUMSY IS AS CLUMSY DOES

Of current interest to practically no one except the tackle companies, who may be on the verge of paying a dividend, I have taken more than a casual interest in fly-fishing.

This carries more than its fair share of hilarity to those fortunate enough to have seen me swing a golf club, trap gun, or plug rod. The very thought of me cocooned in yards of leader and fly line is the very essence of humor: a combination of the possible with the very likely.

Fly-fishing is kind of funny anyway, except to those participants who are working diligently toward the day when they can spend several hours on the stream with the real possibility of not hooking themselves. Hooking something else—like a fish—is a future dream; self-protection is the first level of hoped-for skill.

You've no doubt noticed that most fly-fisherman wear a hat that comes down in the back over the ears and the neck. You have also noticed that all fly-fishing rain gear has an attached hood. Now, if you ask a fisherman why he affects such protective fencing, he, without a smidgen of regard for the truth, will tell you that he wants to protect his neck from the sun. Do you see Arnold Palmer or Jack Nicklaus—who actually spend most of their time in the sun—wearing such stuff? Of course not. The truth is, as you already suspected, that it is infinitely more comfortable and easy to remove a No. 16 Henryville Special from a hat or a hood than from a neck or an ear.

The average fly-fisherman is more concerned with self-defense than a light-heavyweight. And he should be. What little I've done has proven that the immutable law of sport, "If anything can go wrong it will," is right there hovering over you all the time. If you are a right-handed caster, rest assured that the wind always blows from right to left. If you have progressed to where you can often cast as far as 45 feet, most of the rising fish will be 50 feet away. You will seldom have the pattern fish are feeding on, and if you do it will be either too big or hung up in a willow on the second cast. Fly-fishing is like everything else we enjoy. It's harder than it looks, requires unlimited equipment, and the rewards are insignificant and hard to come by. It requires the three skills our Maker was most stingy with: manual dexterity, coordination, and patience.

So then, what does a man say when he returns from the pleasures of the stream bloody of neck and ear, wet of hip and thigh, and so trembling from fatigue, cold, and frustration that his Queen Bee pours him strong drink? He has a choice: A—the truth—which is that he likes fishing catalogs, waders, boxes of flies, jackets crammed with tools and festooned with odds and ends of gear. He likes early-morning breakfasts with his buddies, streamside chitchat, the quiet, and fooling around in the water. Or B—that fly-fishing is relaxing and healthy; it's an inexpensive way to spend a day out-of-doors; catching fish is cheaper than going to the market.

He naturally, being a fisherman, says "B." His wife, naturally, being a wife, translates that into "A," but says nothing. He, pleased at her understanding, decides that she ought to have some of the fun of fishing herself, and makes a silent vow to buy her a fly vise and dressing material for her birthday.

And that is a short summary of how it happens to be in my house. I wish you the best of the season and hope that your wife is as good at tying Woolly Worms and caddis as she is at reloading for trap and skeet.

WIND KNOTS AND WET FEET

I'm a fly-fisherman. You've seen me in a long canoe fishing the Restigouche for Atlantic salmon. Or in a flat-bottomed skiff poled along the flats of Florida stalking bonefish. We've stood side by side in sleet on opening day on the Beaverkill—and in snow at the tag end of things on the Madison. We've argued steelhead flies on the Babine, brown trout methods on the Père Marquette.

You've seen me popping for bass in Georgia and heard me bragging about wet-fly bream in Tennessee. And when they're running—be it shad or stripers—I'll do my best to be there. Unless I'm out for tarpon, or blues—or brookies.

I love those long, slender sticks and all the stuff that goes with them—waders and wet feet not excepted.

I've got four of everything except flies, where I do a little better than that. And reels and rods and matching lines, just in case.

My vest weighs ten pounds, and I never have all the stuff along that I need. I'm an authority on high water, low water, bad tides, and wind knots.

I'm never convinced I've got on the right fly—unless there's a fish attached—which is seldom. I know everything there is to know about landing fish—except when I get too excited to remember—which is always.

I can't double-haul, tie more than two knots, or recognize much more than a mayfly.

But I'm a fly-fisherman. I like the quiet company of pelicans, ospreys, wood ducks, and squirrels. I like the too-rare satisfaction of a perfect cast, the singsong of a running reel, and the etching of a fish against the sky. I like catching the same fish the second or third time more than catching him first. I like to hold him in my hand—then let him go.

But I don't catch much, to be honest—and I honestly don't care. I can be snagged, skunked, sunburned, or partially sub-merged—and still smile. If you don't think I'm crazy—you're a fly-fisherman too.

CHRISTMAS TREES

I've learned to live with a lot of planted things—trout, quail, pheasant, rabbits, and the like—but somehow I resent "planted" Christmas trees. Even my own.

Christmas loomed large to us when I was a boy. Not only to the youngsters, but to everyone else. The end of Thanksgiving marked the beginning of the countdown to December 25th. The pie barrels that were emptied in November began to be filled again, and the pungent fogs of cinnamon, clove, nutmeg, and allspice (even rum or brandy, if you weren't a Methodist) drifted around the corners of the kitchen, as fruitcakes and pies of all descriptions, except the dreaded green tomato kind, were prepared for the holiday season.

Mothers and aunts and grandmothers, even certain sisters, had secret knitting and crocheting projects that were hurriedly stuffed into handy pillowcases when overly prying eyes came drifting by. Fathers and uncles and grandfathers spent their evening hours behind closed doors in the barn and workshops, and only the exquisite fragrances of wood shavings and varnish gave any clues as to what was going on inside.

You could always make a pretty shrewd guess, but most of us didn't—because that would take the fun out of the whole thing. The fact that certain aunts were famous for their luxurious mufflers, and certain grandmothers for mittens with ducks on the back, was sort of forgotten from the year before in the interest of mutual pleasure from the giver to the given. The fact that certain men were celebrated for their crafting of homemade knives or little chairs or red wagons was also ignored in the greater interest of Christmas-morning delight.

I was known in my family as "a good boy, even if he don't pay enough attention," which could be translated as some kind of a dreamer, or one not to be trusted with anything that required manual dexterity, a long span of attention, or good tools. In other words, I was just the right one to pick out the Christmas tree. I had an eye for symmetry, my own hatchet (the one with all the nicks in the edge), and was always fooling around in the woods anyway. We took our Christmas tree pretty seriously, so it gave me a sense of accomplishment to pick one out that pleased everybody.

The tree had to be about as high as I could reach with my outstretched arm—maybe a little higher. Bigger around than I could reach—by a lot. And not *too* full—so we could hang all sorts of things on the branches. Already you can see that this was the kind of job that required a lot of time spent in survey—with Jeff, my rabbit beagle, along for company, and my 20-gauge single shot along for the pot.

Cedar was not allowed because it wouldn't hold the needles, and it was prickly. Pine needles didn't last too long either and turned brown. So the choice was between hemlock or spruce—with hemlock my favorite, because I just felt hemlock was more like a real Christmas tree should be: soft, fragrant, and gentle.

I also was responsible for locating large quantities of ground pine for homemade wreaths, and berries for color—except that bittersweet was forbidden because that was a favorite of the birds when the heavy snows covered everything else.

You realize that Christmas trees, like everything else, are always better "a little farther along." And long miles were searched out for the ideal, with little or no thought for the realistic fact that the farther from home the tree is cut, the harder the job sledding it back where it is wanted. I don't suppose I really cared. The important thing was the *perfect* tree. A tree that everyone stood around and admired, with lovely fragrant aunts mussing your hair and saying, "Where did you *ever* find such a tree?" Implying that only you had the courage and daring to venture where no Christmas-tree hunter had ever been before and had plucked this jewel from an unknown land.

Nowadays, such sweet satisfactions are almost unknown to most of us. You can't just go cut a tree from the back woodlots because they are now covered with some sort of dwellings. You can't go and cut someone else's because that's stealing, and there's something very distasteful about stealing a Christmas tree—it's just the wrong thing at the wrong time of the year.

No, you have to go buy one. Or cut one you've planted a few years ago that has probably by now assumed the stature of a pet. I've done both, and neither leaves me "joyful and rejoicing." I've bought, at incredible prices, the so-called "balled and burlapped" trees that can theoretically be planted later on to add to the beauty of your yard. But you and I know that a properly balled and burlapped tree big enough to grace and scent a decent part of the front room will leave you with a bilateral hernia instead of a merry Christmas if you try to move it without a forklift.

However, at the proper time, carefully braced with eggnog, my tattered checkbook, and my children, I now find myself in the shopping center parking lot—stumbling around a pitch-dark stand of trees intentionally grown for profitable slaughter like hogs or beef. The girls pick out what they hope to be the least damaged of the lot, and we all wrestle it into the back of the wagon.

Christmas being Christmas, our tree, finally strategically covered with tinsel, ornaments, Santas, candy canes, and twinkling lights, manages to assume an attitude of cheer. And in a day or two even I become fond of sitting in the closing dark and watching the play of lights across its boughs.

I dearly love Christmas still. My kitchen pleasures my overromantic memories of long-lost delights with heavy draughts of cinnamon and chocolate and cloves and rum and brandy. A lot of the women I know still knit with love and tired fingers. And now and then I still imagine I can smell wood shavings and varnish.

But how I long for a sullen December afternoon, dragging a Flexible Flyer sled on a long piece of clothesline, with a nicked hatchet slapping my hip. Old Jeff poking his snow-covered nose under rabbitless brushpiles, and the fresh-cut smell of hemlock right behind me filling every breath as I whistle "Tannenbaum, O Tannenbaum." It's a little off key, as I remember, but both Jeff and I felt very merry, and it didn't seem too important that neither one of us was perfect.

"JUST ONE MORE"

One of the things incumbent on me to do is to occasionally lunch with one of the editors of a magazine I write for—sort of noblesse oblige. Well, to make a short story long, I was sitting at the table across from Dave Petzal, listening with breathless fascination as he described each and every shot of a recent 100-straight at trap.

As he neared the end of his story, he suddenly stopped and began sobbing almost hysterically into his napkin. I motioned the waiter to refill Dave's iced tea and then held the glass to his trembling lips as he took a few sips to get control of himself.

"I'm a sick man," he said. "Last week when you and I were going to have lunch and you had to cancel, I went out on the street and seemed to black out. When I came to my senses again I discovered that I'd bought another .300 Weatherby Magnum, taken it to Griffin & Howe, and ordered a new stock with 24-line checkering and all sorts of fancy stuff, including an engraved bolt handle."

"There's nothing wrong with a man treating himself to a little goody now and then," I told him (my voice as calming and reassuring as I could make it).

"You don't understand," Dave whispered in shame, "that's my eighteenth custom rifle. I can't control myself anymore. And what's worse, I think my sickness—and that's what it is—is spreading out into shooting jackets and may go as far as trap guns."

The minute Dave mentioned shooting jackets and trap guns, I'm afraid I paled. The situation was a lot more serious than I'd thought. Having been through this thing once or twice before, I've never really known of a man being completely cured. I generously let Dave pay the luncheon check, put him in a taxi, and gave instructions to the driver that under no amount of pleading should he deliver Petzal anywhere but directly to his office.

The more I puzzled over Dave's problem, the more I realized that it wasn't just Dave whom I had to find some way to help. There are thousands of men just like him in this country who have no one to turn to. But, happily, I think I've got a solution. When a man reaches the point where he no longer has any control over himself, he gets in touch with our central office. For a small fee we catalog every gun he owns, all of his shooting jackets, right down to the cut and the fabric, his knives, and so on—and put them into a computer. The man is sent a bracelet that bears an enameled script reading: *Warning: I am a sports-equipment addict. Before selling me anything, please call: 123-4567* (here we insert the actual phone number of our local central office).

Naturally, the shop owner will see the bracelet and call us. If we discover that the addict is trying to purchase his third 7mm Remington, for example, we talk to him on the phone and try to bring him back to reality. I have instituted an experimental study, using Petzal and several other incorrigible acquaintances as samples, and so far it seems to be working.

We've only had one problem. One of the men managed to employ a friend to pick up his 53rd hunting knife. And when we confronted him with the fact that we'd found out about it, he thanked us for our vigilance—but admitted that he was trying to place an order for a fawn-colored suede shooting jacket with a firm in Madrid under an assumed name. He vowed he would make every effort to have the jacket order cancelled. Then, alas, I found out that the jacket was a size 44. I told him that he could let the order stand and I'd take it myself, since every one of my suede trap coats is more of a chestnut tending toward dark brown.

SHOTGUNNERS ANONYMOUS

I think—perhaps it's only an idle dream—that I will no longer devote most of my waking hours to devising ways to get my hands on another gun.

I've come to recognize collecting as a form of undiagnosed disease. Like the alcoholic who thinks he can just have one and he'll be fine, the gun collector kids himself by saying, "Okay, I've got it all figured out. I'll get just this one last Krieghoff, maybe an extra barrel for handicap, and that will be that, I'll be done with it." But one Krieghoff, he soon discovers, leads to a Model 12, and the Model 12 leads to a 3200, which leads to a Perazzi. His family is impoverished, his children are forced to drop out of college, and when the man comes to shut off the electricity he is asked if he thinks that, in the long run, a modified barrel will be as good for 16-yard targets as an improved modified. And the evenings now

spent in darkness are filled with dreams of unseen treasures . . .
Bonehills, Cashmores, William Evanses, and rare Woodwards.

You want to know, of course, how I—a notoriously weak person when it comes to this sort of self-indulgence—have managed to put the brakes to my self-created juggernaut. Well, it wasn't easy, to say the least. At first, I tried the basic cure—selling a gun in order to ease the pangs of having to buy another one this month. I then rationalized that I had the money, an empty space in the gun rack—I was entitled, indeed forced, to replace the gun I'd sold. I figured, and this is the theory, that I would finally be glutted with the need to shop, bargain, and find excuses to acquire something that virtually duplicated something I already had. But this didn't work. Not only did I get a new gun, but I'd shortly get homesick or lonesome for the gun I'd sold in order to get a new one. I missed my old love at the same time I was patting a new honey. Clearly, the man who comes to shut off the electricity was not too far away.

Next, I went the way a lot of people do when they quit smoking. So many smokes this week, so many fewer the next week, and lo and behold, finally no smokes at all.

I would only get guns at the beginning of a new season. Doesn't that make sense to the well-known Rational Man? (Who exists, by the way, only in the abstruse minds of political theorists.) Of course it does, but the diseased mind is not rational. The sane man divides his year into the ordinary, organized areas, accepted by every gunner. Trap season, skeet season, bird-hunting season—the little bit of overlapping can be as incidental and as lightly taken as a brief skiff of snow on the first day of spring. But not the afflicted collector. I found, even fought against—but helplessly—the fact that I could ring in turkey season (spring and fall), dove season, live-pigeon-shooting season, and that skeet season covers four different gauges, and trap season could be broken down into three separate events.

And as if to offer a drowning man a shove under in deep water, my local gun club installed a Crazy Quail—for which I had no special gun—yet.

My wife mentioned that the end of the house where I stored my guns was beginning to sag the foundation. I bought a van so I could make sure I had two guns available for any event that might occur at any given shoot. My children began worrying how they would do their homework without electric lights. The deep enjoyment I once felt in poring over gun lists and catalogs just before I went to sleep began to diminish under this constant harassment.

I was beginning to weaken, or as my family said, come to my senses, when I began to force them to come along on my visits to gun shops. The sound of their shuffling bare feet in the background and the rustle of their tattered clothes often acted as strong restraint against the lure of a near-mint Webley & Scott or a practically original C Grade Parker. And I found that I frequently left the store having bought nothing more than another box of cleaning patches and another quart bottle of Hoppes.

Risking the scorn of my fellows, I began showing up at the gun club with only two trap guns, and only one skeet gun (one in each gauge, of course).

Then I noticed that my averages were getting a little better. Where before I didn't care how I shot (after all, I was only trying a new gun), I began to take an interest in what I was shooting in terms of score.

I began to realize that a lot of men I genuinely liked couldn't tell a Perazzi from a Fabri at a distance of 30 yards; some even quite a bit less. Many didn't recognize the different engraving masters—the subtleties of a Pachmayr or a Markel or a Galezzi or Kuloch were beyond them. Moreover, they didn't even care!

My absence caused a few gun shops to send "Get Well" cards to the house, and one even sent a "Deepest Sympathy" note to my wife.

I felt a welcome sense of relief when I sent a check to the light company, and I took great pride in the sight of my children wearing new shoes. I knew I was returning to normality when I could sit down and watch television without a cleaning rod and oil can by my side.

I resisted the age-old impulse to celebrate my wedding anniversary by getting a new trap gun for my wife, and I stopped referring to her as "a 14-inch, 1¼, Monte Carlo" when shopping for a new sweater for her and the salesgirl asked her size.

But the great sense of freedom didn't strike home until last summer when I was in London for a day. I did not go immediately to Holland & Holland, Purdey, or a single one of the famous gun shops. Walk by them? Yes—but I did not go in. My wife reminded me that it was Sunday when we arrived and they were all closed, but I knew that in my heart I had found a new strength. I took the Monday morning plane without a real regret.

It would be foolish to say I'll never buy another gun, or sell one, or trade around just a little. The world's greatest easy mark is no longer the pushover he used to be, no sirree Bob! But if you know of where I could get my hands on an old Model 21 in 16 gauge, bored about improved and modified with a straight-hand stock and checkered butt, at the right price, of course, you know where you can reach me. Just don't call me at home, if you can manage it—and if a lady answers, hang up.

ANNUAL REPORT II

Once again it's time for my Annual Report. If you'll recall, last year I had promised to open the meeting with my locally famous feeding chatter, but once more my duck call has been inadvertently misplaced. [Sounds of disappointment from the audience.]

We have incurred about $200 worth of casual losses in the fishing tackle department, due to the increased interest in my youngest daughter's attitude toward angling. Chances are that a good deal of this equipment is in her room. Bigfoot may be living there too, for all anyone knows, and if he is, he's safe from discovery.

Other capital losses include two fly boxes dropped in New Brunswick's Miramichi River; one rod tip broken while trying to dislodge a No. 12 fly from a 4/0 tree branch, one pair of waders in a final teething spasm by Josephine, my would-be retriever; and a miscellany of pipes, shooting glasses, gloves, hats, and lighters that disappear with the same mysterious regularity at gun clubs as my good hunting socks do in the wash. The Chairman, in her unimaginative way, puts these losses down to carelessness, casually dismissing the likelihood of extraterrestrial forces that we as yet know nothing about.

Trivial but troublesome problems continue to beset the Corporation: Deer continue to more than decimate the garden; squirrels continue to disdain their traditional nesting places in preference to my attic; and the Labradors persist in entering the house through the screen on the screen doors. The Chairman continues to resist the idea that these are universal problems beyond my personal control, so I will shortly institute a Research and Construction program, using time and funds previously set aside for more universally beneficial programs such as encouraging the growth of trap and skeet in the neighborhood.

The wood ducks once more have ignored my nesting boxes, but I judge this to be more than offset by the continued growth in the breeding of Canada geese on the pond. The expenditure of flies by my daughters catching panfish in the pond roughly equals the cost of eating fish in a decent restaurant, so I will consider this investment and return as a self-liquidating item. There were no substantial profits or losses above the cost of shooting in either trap or skeet in the past year. As good as my word, I have virtually ceased wagering on the outcome of any given day's shooting, especially shoot-offs. Regrettably, I must note that our average has not increased to anywhere near what I consider my true ability. The Chairman has exercised her veto on several guns that were not only prime investments toward our future financial security, but, I am convinced, would have gone a good way toward solving those vexing problems of low house Five and high Three. A minor change in the bylaws that will result in "one person, one vote" should see a change in this whole situation in the coming year.

The new federal laws involving the use of steel shot have forced the purchase of a new waterfowl gun; a lengthy discussion with the Chairman over safety, deterioration of a capital investment, and a detailed explanation of choke boring, patterns, and the residual energy of No. 4 shot was effected throughout the selection period. (A certain weakness on her part for roast goose and mallard breasts played no small part in these long negotiations.)

No other gun purchases are contemplated at the moment. One trade was effected—a little-used automatic field gun was traded for a new 6-weight trout rod and fly line to match. I realize that the balance sheet shows several rods for 6-weight lines, but this particular rod is a new design virtually guaranteed to improve line control, and promises to more than justify its acquisition in the reduction of leader and fly losses.

You will notice under the heading of Capital Equipment the sale of our reloading machine. This is due in part to a score of 34 in a 50-bird match of some importance; but also to the fact that the workings of the machine far exceeded my grasp of its mechanical principles; and to the circumstance of the friend who constantly repaired it having moved to Virginia. Steps will be taken to replace this necessary tool, but only after considerable market research on my part. (Hopefully this will be concluded in time for me to feature it in my Christmas gifts for the Chairman.)

On the more positive side, I am delighted to report that the covey of quail that lived out by the garden has returned. (The Chairman noted that they really never wandered off, but that I am too deaf from shooting to hear them unless I step on one.) The cornfield has been dotted with young pheasants all fall, and the pond has produced several bass over four pounds. (Honesty compels me to report that two of these fell to a six-year-old neighbor who has mastered the art of the plastic worm, and the others to my nearest relatives while fishing for bluegills with my good trout flies.)

The annual Texas quail hunt was preceded by an unheard-of mix of rain and snow, reducing my already meager chances for limiting out (for once in my life) and added about 20 miles of footwork to the hunting day. To complete the picture, I must tell you that my gunning buddy is absolutely one of the finest shots I have ever seen, and had a series of what must have been his best days. I did not.

The long-looked-forward-to trip to New Brunswick, Canada, for salmon virtually paralleled the trip to Texas. I arrived there after 19 consecutive days of rain. It was almost impossible to get to the river, much less try to fish it. Disappointed? Yes. Surprised? No. A hastily planned second trip to the same area a month later managed to produce enough fish to keep my interest thriving for another year, but just barely. No attempt has been made, nor will there ever be any sort of cost-accounting in regard to fishing or hunting trips. I realize that it is not an orderly procedure to throw most of our annual expenditures in a lump sum categorized as Miscellaneous, but I must remind the Corporation that I was not chosen because of my mathematical wizardry or normality of habit.

Which brings us to another subject. I know you all looked forward to seeing my slides of the salmon-fishing trip, but due to the fact that the Chairman neglected to remind me to check my camera, I forgot to put in a roll of film. I realize how disappointed you all are, but I will make up for this at the next meeting by bringing some slides of various trap shoots as well as some fishing pictures, as I rarely make such a major mistake twice.

I expect a slight increase in spending for the coming year, as each of the girls has decided to take up trapshooting. Having been prudent enough to own more than one or two trap guns, I have been able to make a transfer from existing stock to them. Minor gunsmithing charges will ensue, but other than new wardrobes, head to toe, and various accessories, I expect to launch this endeavor with less cash outlay than a private plane would cost. All in all, it will end up with two more trilling voices saying that I ought to keep my head on the stock . . . etc., etc.

I think I've covered all the major items of our Annual Report. Those wishing to stay a while longer can hear in detail, shot by shot, how I scored a 98, or my theories on salmon fly selection. After all, since I can't show you my slides, I do want you to go home with some kind of useful information.

OPERATION CASE

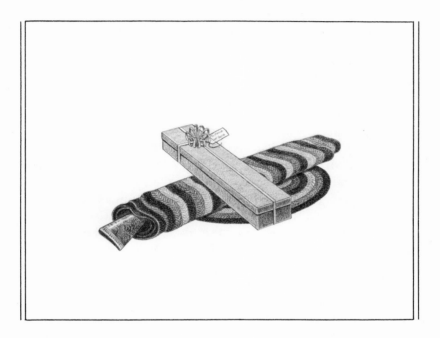

I've just had one of the most beneficial and rewarding trap lessons in years of hanging around gun clubs and listening to my betters carry on. Most advice, as you know, is as transient as a rainbow: it looks good for a few minutes, then it disappears. But this is solid stuff: beneficial to us all and, like all really great ideas, simplicity itself.

As we all know, the real, 24-karat answer to improving our shooting is another gun. The question as to which gun to buy is not nearly as important as the question our wives ask (questions, really) about *why*. Although my wife does shoot trap, I've never been able to engage her in a real evening of trapshooting talk. By that I mean discussing millimeters of pitch-down, toe-out, castoff, forcing cone relief, hammer dwell, coil springs versus leaf springs, and the like—the sincere kind of stuff that will eventually, with its mastery, raise our 16-yard average from 89 to 91. So it's futile to conceive that we can justify to her, as we can to ourselves, that the addition of a new high-rib single barrel is the answer we have been searching for for years. The problem is adding it to the odd gun here and there that we already own, wherein my newly acquired lesson comes in at about 1,250 feet per second.

I said it was simple, and it is, but don't let its simplicity lull you into ignoring it. As we all know, there is shortly going to be a nationwide shortage of gun cases, especially long ones. And as we all know, gun cases are cheap—especially when empty. And as we also all know, the average wife doesn't go around dusting a corner full of gun cases. Nor does she go around lifting them to see which ones are full and which ones are not. I firmly believe that if you came home now and then, threw a gun case on the pile, and said: "Three bucks at a garage sale—be worth six, maybe ten in a few months," the Light of Your Life would smile in conspiratorial agreement with your brilliant assessment of a relatively unknown bonanza, and might even go so far as to encourage the acquisition of more. Will this same lady then ask you hard questions when you go to the gun club with half a dozen cases in your car? She will not. Will she ask you if one of them contains the latest adjustable-choke model? She will not. What she *will* do is gradually become accustomed to your having a dozen or so gun cases lying around waiting for the market to get just right. But don't raise your average too quickly—or too high—she might get suspicious!

Operation Case works as well or better with new fly rods. While the shortage of aluminum tubing for fly rods may not have reached the degree of interest to become a topic at the ladies' Thursday shoot or bridge game, it is, at your insistence, reaching a serious level. Again, as with the gun cases, she will not rummage around them. No doubt the average wife of more than five years' residence can lift your wallet off the dresser and know instinctively that it contains three twenties rather than three tens, but she cannot lift a rod case and know that the contents are not a Cheap City glass rod but the Orvis Madison 5-weight you've coveted for years, or the Scientific Anglers new graphite which you've needed to teach the steelhead a lesson.

Of course you have to be careful about carrying all this too far. Any judge in the country will listen more than attentively to a distraught woman who complains that her husband has a collection of 1,000 empty gun cases in the attic or a two-car garage full of aluminum-rod tubes, and has long ceased to notice when she's wearing a new apron and barely says "Thank you" when she's done an especially nice job of patching his waders or touching up the paint on the decoys.

Ed Zern and I once cooked up a scheme (pure genius!) whereby we would exchange gifts at appropriate times of the year: waders, fly boxes, cases of trap loads, shooting coats, and the like. But Ed got so excited about it all that he told his Labrador, who then told mine, and the first thing we knew, it was all over and done with.

A while back you could, if you were judicious to a fault, claim that the new 3-inch magnum was the raffle prize at the D.U. dinner. But now that women have caught on for the most part to using the telephone, and chatting away time that would be better spent making venison jerky or knitting camouflage sweaters, the lines of communication have been drawn against us.

I tried for quite a while to restrict my wife's reading to shotshell ballistics and reloading formulas, with several fine fly-tying manuals for a change of pace. What I didn't want her poring over were the annual catalogs from Orvis, L. L. Bean, Eddie Bauer, and other major suppliers of basic necessities. Now and then I'd find an old magazine and tear out an ad and discuss the change in consumer costs with her. "Look at this, Mrs. Hill!" I'd explain while she was busy cleaning the lantern chimneys, "The new Parker double has gone from seventy-five dollars up to a hundred and ten!"

"Goodness," she'd say, "maybe I ought to go back to raising chickens so we can save egg money—before you know it, they'll be going up again. I think I can get another year or so out of my kitchen ax, and a touch of solder will make my scrubboard as good as new."

I even tried getting mail delivered to a box number at the post office, and leaving the house in my old gunning coat, putting the new one on in the car, and changing again when I got home. But she was in the habit of checking my stuff to see how her mending and patching held up, and after a bad glass or two of cider, I forgot to change, and that ruined the whole scheme. And then the companies got the computer thing going, and instead of getting my catalogs at the office, it seems as if every other mail has one coming into the house.

Zern tried for a time to completely restrict his hunting and fishing companions to those who wore his exact size and used guns with his exact measurements. But what he forgot, being Zern, was that he was left-handed, and all the shoulder patches, bolt actions, etc., were on the wrong side, and the scheme wouldn't hold together.

Lord knows what would happen—and I shudder to think of it—if we were honest and admitted that we made over $5,000 a year and could actually afford a new gun every so often. The first thing you know, there'd be strangers all over the house installing electricity and plumbing. Your wife would be pestering you about getting a new car with a self-starter instead of a crank, and I can't imagine, and won't even try, to guess where it would end—if it ever did.

Women don't know what's good for them. You, being mindful of their health and beauty, point out that the rosy complexion they once were so proud of came in large part from the fresh air and exercise they got chopping wood for the kitchen stove and drawing water for their weekly bath. You can't paint on that look from the outdoors with powder and rouge—and the last time I looked, they weren't exactly giving that stuff away either!

If you do try the empty-case method—and you should—take a look in the attic where your wife stores all those boxes she saves from Christmastime. Shake a few; open some of them up. You might just find that getting a new single-barrel or Orvis rod into the house isn't going to be quite as difficult as you thought!

WHAT IS WILDERNESS?

One of my Labradors believes that when she climbs up on my bed she can, by merely closing her eyes, become invisible. I've always admired that sort of belief—that by thinking a situation to be so, it becomes so.

Take the concept of wilderness: what is it really? Is it that little while on a mountain ledge when no jet engine noise is heard, no contrail overhead telling you that other men are passing by? I think so—and, after all, the choice is no longer ours to make. Since the physical presence is obvious, we have to shut it out, turn our back—and close our eyes.

Wilderness can be the chunking of a canoe through the rip of heavy white water—even if it's in sight of a highway. Wilderness can be that sudden enchanted muffling of forest sounds that happens with a fresh falling of snow . . . even when your deer stand is just barely two miles from where you parked your car.

Wilderness can be truly the "back of beyond." Or it can be where church bells are still faintly heard. Working with an ax in my woodlot is a little, momentary brushing with it—the sound of my blade thunking is just as comforting to me as an early Dakota Territory homesteader's was to him. Each of our wildernesses being an act of faith, a belief, a thing of the soul and the willingness to accept it, often independent of the physical removal from the familiar.

As a British scientist (who would agree with us) put it, "If the facts do not agree with the theory, so much the worse for the facts."

We must have our little wildernesses, no matter what size they are, no matter where they would in reality sit on a map.

Wilderness, when you're hungry for it, can start almost anywhere. It's that invisible line we cross from the everyday to the out-of-the-ordinary. It can be seeing, with great satisfaction, the evening gathering of heavy clouds and feeling the bite of a northeast wind as you pile stuff into the car on the way to a duck camp. Wilderness is knowing for sure that the pheasant in your corn patch is absolutely as wild as, or maybe wilder than, its cousins that are still roaming China. Wilderness is the feeling that closes your throat and starts a dampness around the eyes when some big-going Walker or Redbone starts telling you in his ancient language that he's running fox.

Wilderness is that yearning we always get at the calling of flight birds; it's the feeling of incredible curiosity watching the aimless wanderings of a grizzly or the salmon in his death-searching climbing of almost impassable cascades. There we stand, the wilderness-yearning in us wanting to turn us as wild as they are—or maybe back again to as wild as we ourselves once were.

Wilderness is that odd feeling that comes over us, every once in a while, in some quiet spot: a sensation of sureness, of strength, of an almost-forgotten feeling that we could really cope—we could have made it—anytime, anyplace. We could have walked right along with Boone or Clark. We could have stalked the buffalo and then slept in the robe around the same fire with Bridger or Carson—because we can feel and understand the very same things they did.

Wilderness is understanding something in your guts that you can't analyze with your mind; it's understanding the need to hear the wolf call one more time—and answering him with a message from your heart carried by moonlight: "I am your brother."

Wilderness is the strange comfort that comes on us when we're bone cold, and uncertain at the coming of darkness, and then tracking the heavens for the security of the North Star; we think and comfort ourselves that this knowledge is one that we are, right now, sharing with a thousand years of mankind—a common tracking to whatever place it was called *home*.

I get absolutely starved for quiet, the smell of evergreens, the footfalls and chatter of wild things, the feel of a clean wind. I used to say that I like to go away and solve things, but that's not really so; in truth, I go away to feel . . . to question.

When I was small I had, like all youngsters, a greater awe or wonder brought on by my little wildernesses—like my three-hour trapline or hunting a bee-tree for Grandpa. I would try to imagine what things that giant Norway spruce had seen. What Indian feet had leapt the brook on the very same stones I used to cross? Who was the very first to walk the path that led to the spring that birthed the brook?

Small thoughts, no doubt, but as universal in their narrow compass as the wonder that drove Columbus and Hudson and the countless others, both known and lost, to take the somewhat larger travels than a schoolboy trapline or lining a honeybee.

The same instincts, no matter the degree of venture, still haunt me now. Does it really matter that our footsteps follow where the earlier adventurer went alone and first? Not if we close our eyes and let those intruding facts and long-lost faces turn invisible and disappear—so we can climb up into our wilderness and see only what we want or only what we need to see.

A PENNY SAVED IS
UNLIKELY

After telling my insurance man that I was unexpectedly called out of town and wouldn't return from the Vale of Kashmir for several months, I began mulling over my own version of his Lifetime Investment Plan. Something a bit different from what he had in mind, but a plan, nevertheless, no matter how haphazard or insufficient it might seem to those who plan to be my survivors.

The very word *planning* carries the concept of choice. You ordinarily plan something by balancing it against something else. Let's say you had planned to finally do something about your insurance, then by a stroke of luck you stumble across a fully trained bird dog you've hunted over and like exceedingly well, and the man who's selling the dog is also willing to part with a 16-gauge Parker that you also like. You, wisely, put Plan B into effect, because who knows when a bargain like this will ever turn up again, while Plan

A, the insurance increase, will be around whenever you're ready. You could almost get your wife to agree with this sort of intelligent forward thinking.

A friend of mine, obviously another adherent of our Lifetime Investment Plan theory, was sporting a very, very expensive set of binoculars on a duck hunt we were sharing. With a voice straining with envy, I asked him why in the name of common sense did he part with an exorbitant amount of money when for what would only be an absurd amount he could have gotten a pair of glasses virtually as excellent. "Well," he said, eager to be shut of a long-rehearsed answer, "I figured that over the next twenty years, maybe thirty, the extra two hundred dollars would only come out to ten dollars a year. About a dollar a month. Roughly three cents a day. Now, for a lousy three cents a day, I'd be denying myself something I really want—and that wouldn't make much sense, would it?"

His logic was so clear, so inviolable, so pure, that tears started to well in my eyes. How simple even the Law of Gravity became once Newton explained it. How swiftly we've progressed in flight in the brief 70 years since Orville and Wilbur showed us how it worked at Kitty Hawk.

Only a recluse or an economic isolationist would reject such an incredible and simple mathematical formula. And, no one, even my wife, has ever called me an economic isolationist.

The brochure propounding the actuarial statistics involving my life-span, having been mailed to me over a strong show of indifference on my part, was rummaged out of a large pile of unopened mail. My fingers sped down the list headed *Male, Married* and came to rest at a rather distant prognosis of my life-span. (Married men tend to live longer than single men. You figure *that* out!)

Even my Stone Age mathematical grasp could come up with the few pennies a day that would suffice to clear my gun case of the clunkers and replace them with a couple of engraved sidelocks hand-measured down to the last millimeter of castoff.

Mere pennies! Mere pennies, that's all that was standing between me as I am now and me as I might be—had I only seen the truth sooner. No more would I pick through the half-price rack and try to squeeze myself into a pair of 36-waist brush pants when for mere pennies I could have upland pants made to order.

A handful of coppers a week would find my infantry-broken feet encased in boned calf or elkhide hand-contoured over every callous and bunion.

Just not mailing one letter or so a week could be the piddling difference between my faded work shirts and the soothing influence of Viyella or even cashmere.

However, being not entirely devoid of the confines of common sense, I vowed to stop short of that unforgettable Hollywood description of decadent luxury: "jock straps made of chinchilla, and silk drawers that were envied by stars."

Foremost in my mind was not to let Mrs. Hill in on my little discovery; her turn would come when she needed a new muffler or overshoes. I would take care of the basics I had long dreamed of first, then share the wealth, so to speak.

I called a banker friend of mine who knows how to add, subtract, and divide, and asked him what the difference between buying a $60 glass rod and a $300 cane rod, with two tips and an aluminum case, would come to—in pennies a day—over 12,775 days.

He clicked away at something on his desk and gave me the answer I had only been wise enough to speculate at. I forgot what it was, but it seemed so piddling that I shuddered at my years of ignorant self-denial.

"Take the twelve thousand days as a base to make it simple," I went on, "and give me the same figures for these." And I went through a hastily drawn up list of odds and ends. A safari to Kenya, a side-by-side .458, a matched pair of shotguns, a few hand-tailored whims in Donegal tweed, a live-pigeon shoot in Madrid, a week of salmon fishing in Scotland, some paintings, and a handful of limited-edition books. Just odds and ends, as I said, the first things that came to my mind.

He gave me the answers, each more slowly than the last, then asked me if I'd just won a lottery or something. A trifle smugly, I assume, I told him, "No, I've just come on to something a little bigger than that," and hung up the telephone before he got too curious. This was definitely not the kind of insight you leave around for bankers to mull over.

What it amounted to, as far as I could see, was that I had the sum of a cent a day for 12,000 days, at rock bottom, to play around with. If you had the gray matter to see it that way, and I was one of the blessed who had the stuff now working for him like a computer.

My life-style, while not exactly on the plane of a Bulgarian dirt farmer, was due for a long-awaited lift. As I sorted through the catalogs, I felt the power of a man who has seen the light—I was now one of the few who understand that most mysterious thing we call money. Long-forgotten schoolbook phrases like cartel, leverage, pyramiding, began to fall into my casual conversation. While it was probably too late, chronologically as well as emotionally, for me to amass real wealth, I could at least amass the trinkets—or some of them.

No longer would I be forced to eat humble pie and bum flies, one at a time, from my friends; now I could order them from catalogs—by the dozens. No longer would I have to sit up late at night and live with the insecurity of my own hand-tied leaders—I could order the new knotless ones. No longer would I be subject to the upraised eyebrows of my trap squad as I tilted the barrels to let the shot run out from one of my homemade squibs; I would shoot only factory loads. No longer would I have to stoop to pouring off-brand specials into bottles with more familiar and reliable labels. *Good-bye* to supermarket beer and *hello* to the good stuff seen advertised on TV! There was even a good chance I might pay my dentist bill in a year or so. . . .

What more tragic than to soar to such heights of discovery, thresholds where few men have flown, and suddenly find that your wings were wax and that you must, like most dreamers, awake and tumble to the same earthbound ways-and-means. My bank friend, with whom I occasionally shoot, had mulled, as I feared he might, and figured out what I was up to. He sent me a little note to the effect that if I *saved* a penny a day the first day, two cents the second, three cents the third, and so on, at the end of a year I'd have enough money to do a lot of the things I would never be able to do otherwise. He also remarked that of all the things he considered unlikely, my saving *any* money (his italics, not mine) ranked right up there with life on Mars and little people in flying saucers.

I am not one so stubborn as to argue with this assumption.

Nor, however, am I so easily put off in my search for release from life's bargain basements. I remain convinced that my Lifetime Investment Plan does have some merit. The idea is right, but some details remain to be straightened out. I still have my 12,000 days. I still believe in the theory of "only pennies a day more." The only question is who's going to get the pennies. Right now I suspect it's whoever it is that has the trap gun I can break targets with. I know it's not going to be my insurance man . . . and so for a while also ends the dream of ever being able to pay my dentist.

The idea that "the best is the cheapest in the long run" is right up there with the things I still believe are true—like "the only way to break a hundred straight is one at a time." But when you come to think about it a little, these are sort of parallel statements: mere pennies—mere targets.

And that puts us right back at the beginning: mere me.

ENOUGH IS NEVER ENOUGH

I was completely miserable only three times last year—once lying in a shallow goose pit on my back in two inches of ice water in a sleet storm, once when I went in over my waders trout fishing north of Hudson Bay, and once bird shooting in my shirtsleeves when the temperature dropped about 20 degrees and I was seven miles or so from the car.

I don't count (I can't—they're too many!) emotional miseries. Lost shoot-offs, flies that came untied when I was into a good fish, missed easy shots at geese just after bragging about how nifty I am at incoming overhead birds, days when my fairly well-trained dog either ranged out of sight all day or stayed between my feet. Dumb gun trades, dumb fly rod trades, and all the times I fished when the water was too low, too high, too hot, or too cold. These are just ordinary, everyday facts of life that I have lived with too long to make much of.

(My shaking and shivering during the above-mentioned goose shoot caused one country wit to remark that I looked "like death chewing a dry cracker.")

I fully expect this year to have its share of similar delights: fogged scopes, knots that weren't, bulletproof birds, mysterious disappearances of herds of deer, flocks of geese, and schools of fish. I am trying desperately to reduce equipment revenge to the minimum by using only the simplest sort of stuff. But I won't be completely—or even moderately—successful. Who else do you know that had his hand warmer set him on fire? I have to expect a certain number of things to go wrong; I'm just hoping to stay somewhere this side of disasters.

One of my problems that I can never come to terms with is the fact that I don't know how to fix anything very well. I'm one of America's greatest users of glue and plastic tape—neither of which seems to stick as well for me as advertised. I leave a rather modest, but continual trail of parts across the country. Somewhere in Colorado is the spring from the magazine of my .270. Somewhere in Quebec are two rod tips and a reel handle. Some duck blind is hiding the front bead of my shotgun. I'm not counting the stuff I lose through forgetfulness, like my favorite camouflage cap, or good pipes and lighters, or stuff that breaks because I'm clumsy or careless or inept—like fly hooks broken off on rocks from a sloppy backcast, or lost spoons because I didn't test the line the way I should, or automatics that didn't work because I put the rings in backwards. It's just that a lot of equipment knows that it can get away with stuff with me the same way a horse knows he can do as he damned pleases when I'm aboard. What little vanity I have left forbids any mention of what my shotshell reloads are like . . .

All of this, as I'm sure I've mentioned before, makes me exceedingly careful about the selection of my companions. With few exceptions they know how to match the hatch, start balky outboards, put automatics together, mend broken rod tips, and the like. I, in turn, am extremely flattering in my praise, overly generous when I pour, and give them first crack at birds coming in over the decoys and their favorite seat in the boat. It's only common sense to reserve your best bourbon for gunsmiths and friends who tie flies.

If you're the average gunner and fisherman, I can almost see you nodding in agreement as you remember exactly the same things happening to you. They are as much a part of being out-of-doors as getting caught in rainstorms or leaving the lunch in the car.

One factor in the past year I haven't been able to do much about is traveling by air. I've arrived in the back country of Canada and discovered that my fly rods were left in New York. On another trip my gun case was smashed, and some of the small necessaries kept in it were lost. I was hoping the gun was lost too, since it wouldn't work too well on going-away broadbills or mallard and I had one in mind to replace it with—but my luck only stretches so far. The gun was returned in less than a week.

Another habit the airlines share is not allowing you to carry more than one knife. I like to try and take two. A pocketknife to clean my pipe and for other small chores, plus a hunting or fishing type to clean the catch—if I have to. If you admit to having more than one, they take one away and promise to send it to you; they never have in the times I'm personally familiar with. I thought about this knife thing for a while and came up with what I thought was the perfect answer. I waited until one of my knives was being removed for "security reasons" and then I posed this question to the guard: "When I get on the plane, I'm going to order a steak." He said he hoped I enjoyed it. I said, "When I get my steak, they will bring me a knife to cut it with. A knife longer, sharper than the one you're promising to send back to my home—but you won't." He looked up at me with that official glaze that means they're not going to answer, and shoved me through the line. So much for my quick wit and solid logic. But I keep promising to pose the same question to the next important airline official I meet. I'd also like to find out what they do with the old rusty knives out of all our fishing bags.

I've argued with airline personnel about bringing dogs on board, geese (cleaned and picked) as hand baggage, fly rod cases instead of a coat (they take up the same space in the closet)—and every time I've gotten an argument. The worst one was the dog. There's an involved airline rule about having so many pets on any flight in the passenger compartment: one in each class—if it's a small pet and in some sort of container. I'll agree that's reasonable. I don't want to fly with somebody's 100-pound Labrador trying to get in my lap either. But this particular puppy I wanted to bring along weighed five pounds. I said I would hold it in my lap. I would even hold it in some sort of carton. The airline said *no,* they already had one dog on board. (This, I found out later, was not true.) So I said fine, I'll buy another seat. They sold me one and I marched on the plane, put the puppy (in her provided carton) in the seat next to me, and relaxed. But not for long. Arguments ensued. Voices were raised. Objections pro and con were sustained and overruled. Finally the Captain came out. Looked at the dog. Mentioned the fact he admired the breed, gunned the odd bird when time permitted, and hoped we both enjoyed our flight. Now and then justice and mercy—or common sense—appear on the scene, but I still say the odds are three to five against.

Man is always at the mercy of things he thinks he is close to controlling—but isn't. We simply cannot avoid icy water next to the skin, nor the devious ways of monofilament. We may sometimes find a momentary truce in the war between man and machine—but never a lasting peace. Outsmarted by birds, ignored by feeding fish, driven to near madness by our dogs, and misunderstood by our nonsporting friends, we go forth with the same blind faith and the feeling of "It's not going to be me" as the sinner who weekly listens to vivid descriptions of hell from a preacher.

But maybe that's so much the fun of it all. Maybe it really isn't going to be us . . . but we have to go and find out for sure. It's only a little adventure treading carefully to within a millimeter of the top of the waders, leaving the rain gear at home in the face of a lowering storm, or throwing a shaking leg over a horse named TNT. But where would we be without the kind of days that make us say, "I've enjoyed about as much of this as I can stand."

CHANGES

I hear the sounds of the night in my travels; the love songs of owls.
I hear the thunder of lake ice as it grows thick; the graveside
mourning of coyotes. I hear the snow-crust pattings of rabbit feet as
they waltz under the eyes of the man in the moon; the bark of the
fox who's listening too. I feel the wind pushing me to test my
strength. I hear the old trees fall when their time comes to lie down.

I see the first Christmas rose that works its way up through
the snow. I see where the bear has left its den to check the clock. I
see where the mink and the muskrat have met over a pink spot in
the snow. I know who sleeps, who walks by night, who thrives and
who does not.

I see the rivers being hidden, the mountains turn to ice-cream
cones. I see where the deer hunger, where the elk lets winter turn
him into raven food. I hear the wind asking the weak to rest in its
cold arms.

I am there when the wind softens and lets the river run. I see the first trilliums appear and wonder how they know. I watch the trout slide into the sunlight and fling himself into the air like a speckled scythe. I hear the gossip of mallards telling the world that it's spring . . . as if it didn't know.

I shiver as the yellow fingers of lightning pick through the woods. I believe when the thunder tells me that I have no place to hide. I wonder if this might be the last sound to boom against my ears. I am as frightened as a mouse under a circling hawk.

I watch the river seizing tons of rock and trees and whatever else stands in the way of its need for more running room. I watch a pool die and another being born. Where there is a waterfall drilling solid rock, there I am. The whispering of a spring makes me want water, and, like the thirsty animal I am, I stretch out, belly to the ground, and drink, watching the reflection of the sky—for *something*.

I smell the swamp digesting what it swallowed a thousand years or more ago—birds with leather wings and burning eyes fly still, in my imagination. I inhale the fragrance of skunk cabbage, May apples, and the wild rose—all in one breath.

I stare back at the questing eye of the woodcock I surprise having breakfast. I am fooled by the dragging wing of the grouse as she lures me from the spot where half-a-dozen walnut chicks lie— not quite as still as she would like. I see the doe nuzzling twin fawns to their feet—still glistening wet from where they swam all winter long. I see the silly-looking buck trailing velvet from his tender birthday antlers.

A sullen, most disinterested skunk leads her string of self-miniatures. She does not acknowledge my applause. The Canadas make a quiet honk to be sure that I have seen what a wonderful thing they have done—a battleship at each end of a line of toy boats.

A pickerel stares at me with angry eyes, bravely keeping herself between me and the little unseen inches in the weeds. I look for my favorite at each turn of the river: a brand-new moose all eyes, all ears, all legs, who always looks as if he would come out and play but Momma won't let him.

I hear the silence of possums. The small talk of bitterns and herons. The thrashing of the heavy bass and the tinkling of the minnows they're herding. Tree toads telling tales about their size. The bullfrog saying he's the boss. Voices from everywhere—and again the mallards telling us it's summer . . . as if we didn't know.

I watch the brooks and lakes get down to their everyday business. I study the willow branch I stuck in the earth last year and see, with pride, that it likes it here. I regret the loss of the hollow ash that had so often shown me a wood duck. I roll a rock in the water, hoping I have made a home for a brookie.

I know where the best watercress grows, where the bee tree is, and sassafras and persimmons and strawberries sweeter than kisses. Elderberry, partridge berry, and bittersweet all grow in the garden that is tended by my friends.

I save a quill or two from the moulting geese, count the smaller ones, and note that there are five instead of six. A blue heron stares me away from his fishing hole. If there is an eagle or an osprey, I will see it. I practice my off-key whistled imitation of the Baltimore oriole as one flies by. I hope he's flattered; not because we sound anything alike, but because I think it's pretty. I practice my *bobwhite* for the same reason—with the same result. I quack at the mallards, who keep reminding the world that it's autumn . . . as if it didn't know.

The small raccoons are starting to act serious; walking around all bent over, looking guilty about being caught stealing mussels from the brook. The once-spotted fawns are now the color of cider. The geese no longer honk for my attention. The ospreys have gone. The muskrats are building up the roof. My brook-trout rock is almost covered with water. The pheasants are quarreling over the bedrooms in the meadow roost. Now the quail call is only a lingering postponement of sunset. I hear the elk whistling that there must be more elk; the brown trout running for the creeks to make more browns. The apples are all gone except for the one or two on every tree that forgot to drop.

The doe taps at the ice for her morning drink. Frost makes the meadow squeak under my feet. The evening feeding flock of geese flies a little higher than it used to when it sees me. The beaver are doing more night work—just in case. The last picking goes on; the cornfield is gleaned; the beechnuts are almost all gone, and the possums eye the one last withered persimmon.

The hunter's moon and the northeast wind make me feel wilder. I walk more softly and stop more often. I watch the buck's neck swell as he bends over the sumacs to polish his splendid antlers. There is passion and urgency in the air and I smell it. The mallards are wary and softer-voiced now. They are telling the world that winter is coming on . . . as if it didn't know.

I see and hear everything. I am everywhere. The wilderness and I belong to each other. I am one of its animals. I am one of its hunters.

FREE ADVICE

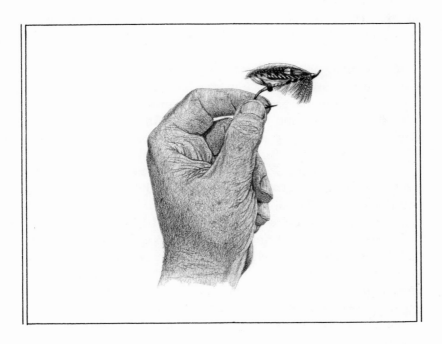

Mr. Gimbel, the department store genius, is reported to have said, "I know only half my advertising works . . . but I don't know which half."

Mr. Hill, unsung, impoverished, and unquoted, feels the same way about the advice he always receives before leaving to go fishing or hunting. Half of it is right . . . more or less, now and then.

My biggest mistakes have come from listening to the self-proclaimed voice of experience—the guy who has been where I'm going. He figures that his three-day weekend at Lake Drear is what the place is all about—all the time. He advises you accordingly: "Don't bother to bring any bug dope; never even saw a mosquito . . . must be all the spraying they do on the trees up there." This immediately alerts me to call Orvis and buy two of their special repellent jackets. Smudge pots for the lodge porch, a half-gallon of

Muskol, head net and gloves. Flypaper, pest strips, and various medicines to reduce the swelling go into my kit. I am not disappointed. I spend the whole time besieged by moose flies, blackflies, mosquitoes, gnats, and for comic relief hold an evening calcutta on the number of tick and chigger bites I've sustained.

"Going up to No Salmon River?" I admit that I am. "Don't bother bringing any waders—hip boots are more than enough . . . spent most of my time casting from the banks wearing bedroom slippers." I instantly pack an extra pair of waders, repair kit, my very short fly vest, and my wading staff. An emergency flotation device is clipped to my jacket, and I make sure my wife knows where the extra copy of my will is kept.

Sure enough, it's been raining there for the past 72 hours, the bridge to the camp has washed out, and you'd need hip boots to go outside to the bathroom.

"Understand you're heading to Coot Marsh for a few ducks?" "You bet!" I answer. "Bring plenty of seven-and-a-half trap loads," he advises. "Those birds pitch right into the decoys like they're on wires. Never had a shot over thirty yards all last season." I put away my pump gun and do an extra special cleaning job on the three-inch magnum auto. The 6s go back on the shelf and out come the heavy 4s—I absolutely *know* that my whole time will be downwind, pass shooting at 50-yard rockets.

It's a simple code to break, as you can see. When a buddy who just returned from Idaho tells you to bring some streamers, a dozen No. 6 muddlers, and a sinking line, you nod, thank him with genuine emotion, and start tying No. 22 Adams, 24 Quill Gordons, and searching around for that spool of 7X tippet material you had somewhere.

ADVICE: Bring a light sweater because it gets a little chilly around evening.
REACTION: Pack a heavy down jacket and long underwear.

ADVICE: Old Cotton's got the gentlest riding horses in Colorado.
REACTION: Wrap one arm in a cast before you leave home and insist that you have to walk 12 miles a day on doctor's orders.

ADVICE: You've never eaten walleyes until you taste the way those Indian guides cook them.
REACTION: Rolaids, bicarbonate of soda, aspirin, and homemade sandwiches.

Obviously the list can go on and on. I know the situations well.

There's the guy who says he'll call you at six in the morning so you can get ready. What do you do? Set two alarm clocks.

Your wife says not to worry, she'll have your good suit out of the cleaners in plenty of time for the D.U. Dinner. Guess what you wear?

The camp writes and says don't bother to bring any shells, they have plenty. Sure they do: if it's a quail shoot, you can have all the heavy 6s you want. If it's a duck camp, you have a choice between 2s or 8s.

"Don't bother to bring a shirt and tie—we're very informal here for dinner." Who's the only guest not wearing a tie besides your Labrador?

It's not that "good advice" isn't well-intentioned, but why does everybody who has spent more than two hours in any given place have to consider himself a qualified expert on the flora, fauna, best places to eat, and what the weather will be at any given time?

Doesn't anybody ever say "I really don't know" any more? Ask a bystander who is watching his very first round of skeet where you were on that low house 5 target you missed, and he'll give you an answer. You don't even have to ask him—he's going to tell you that you lifted your head anyway.

Then there's the other school of which I may soon become a member—those who won't take any advice, at all, no matter what. Example: A testy old man fishing on the Au Sable in Michigan, catching nothing while all around him are wrist-weary from fighting trout. One of the better fishermen asked him what fly he had on, and the old man replied, "A black ant." The expert reminded him that this was March, there was still snow on the ground, and any local black ant with a smattering of brains was deep asleep and would so remain for months—and that the trout hadn't seen a black ant for so long they forgot what they were. The old man dismissed such talk with "I always fish with black ants!"

I would dearly love to have that stern Gary Cooper look that reads "If I want any advice I'll ask for it." But I must resemble a lost and lonely dog whom everyone is determined to feed with tidbits of misinformation—unasked-for, unwanted, unheeded. The guy who constantly comments on my funny casting technique is the same guy who is always hung up in a tree. The guy who criticizes my shooting stance has a personal long-run of eight. The guy who tells me what's wrong with my duck dog doesn't know a golden retriever from a yellow Lab.

Why can't we ever get someone whose advice and help we would welcome with tears in our eyes to talk to us? Like the rest of the world of "average" skills, I believe—along with you—that someday a Superstar will put his hand on my shoulder and say, "I've been watching you and you're a natural . . . all you have to do is just change your gun point like this (and he demonstrates—and I understand it for once) and you've got it made." And there I am running 100 straights the way I always knew I could all along.

My casting stroke would draw crowds at the practice pool, my skeet scores would become legends, and proud fathers would point me out to their sons.

Well, this may be the stuff that dreams are made of—but reality will find me pinned in the far corner of the cocktail party, nodding in helpless agreement to some illiterate telling me what's wrong with a certain column called Hill Country, written by what's-his-name.

TALISMANS

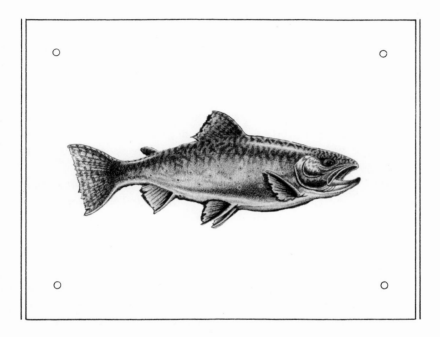

Among my boxes of odds and ends, I have one that holds a small collection of very ordinary little stones. A collection, like many of our odd quirks, that is based part on superstition and part on wishful thinking. Supposedly, there's a legend (and I still like to believe in legends) that if you carry a stone away from a river, you'll return to put it back.

I see no good reason why the same wishful thinking won't work as well on a pinecone from an elk canyon in Colorado, a partridge berry from a woodcock cover in Pennsylvania, or a scrub oak gall from a long-remembered deer hunt in the lovely Texas river country—even my pintail feathers from a never-to-be-forgotten day in Utah.

I'm a great believer in good luck (as opposed to a hard worker honing what ought to be the necessary skills), and if simple little things like crossing my fingers or tossing a pinch of salt over my left shoulder have stood the test of time, who am I to argue? Somehow this reminds me of the great French writer Voltaire, who on his deathbed was asked to renounce the devil. Voltaire thought about this for a minute and wisely replied, "This is no time to make enemies."

Most of us have a lucky hat we like for trapshooting or a favorite sweater for the goose blinds. Who wants to tempt fate? The riskiest thing a man ever does is marry, and who among us has a bride who didn't wear "something borrowed, something blue." How about when the guy next to you runs a 25 straight, and you remark that he shot pretty well; he, modestly (!), replies that he was lucky—and you, in turn, answer that you'd as soon be lucky as good.

As a matter of curiosity, if you're curious, the word *lucky* first appeared in the English language about the year 1600. And, it will come as no surprise to us, that one of the first written uses of it is: "It hath been my luck always to beat the bush while another kild the hare." Such is the attitude of sportsmen since the beginning of recorded time and such will it ever remain.

The things we wear for luck, like our time-tested hats and sweaters, as you know, were called talismans when the Crusaders and medieval knights wore similar touches—scarves from their ladyloves or religious trappings of one sort or the other. And the word *talisman* had its roots in the old Arabic word for a man of great learning. So, if it was smart then for a jousting knight to sport a favorite scarf to help him keep from being pierced by lance or hacked by sword, I figure the principle is still sound in our modern-day adaptation.

Our little superstitions have a kinder place as well. For instance, when you've missed your 24th bird and the guy who beat you says "That was a bit of bad luck," what he really means is that you messed it up as usual. And should you ever get into the shoot-off and your opponent wishes you good luck, what he really means is that you'll need it—and plenty of it.

A whitetail rack we've saved, or a mounted duck or fish, often represents to us something different than it does to other people. I've got a scuffy-looking woodcock hanging from a string that I treasure—not for the bird itself, but more because it was the first bird that my now-lost Tippy and I had taken together. And when I look at this, it's not the bird I see so much as a merry black pup working tenuously around the corner of a little swamp, all a bundle of surprise and wonder and excitement at the flush, and then the sudden coming of understanding when the bird was downed and brought to hand. My few white-tailed deer are nothing special in the way of spread, but one, a single horn shaped like a Y, recalls a hunt with my father in the bitter cold. I keep it only as a token of a time that I don't want ever lost or forgotten.

And so it goes. A stone, a leaf, a feather—each a dream or wish or story that we like to have for reasons of our own. An eccentricity perhaps, but as old as time—a little way to bring a special something back.

I know that there are a lot of things I wish I'd saved, or did, and for a time thought lost. Mostly little things you tuck away and find they turn up later when you don't expect them with their nice surprise. A day-saving trout fly offered by a stranger on a stream, snapshots left between the pages of a misplaced book, an empty shell that tells a mule deer story, a duck call with imprints of a puppy's teeth. Or a row of collars hanging in the barn to keep in touch with dogs since gone away.

The list is long and endless, but the reasons are about the same. We never know about tomorrow's turn, it only lives in hope; but a yesterday can be rerun almost at will, and keeping our little talismans is a way of hoping they will repeat themselves—my rocks from the river, your flies and collars, are like the prayer wheels or the beads of the faithful, who by merely touching them fill themselves with fresh belief in all good things.

As long as our lives are full of little corners where we can rest and visit a little wherever we like, with whomever we want to recall—rummaging through the little boxes of odds and ends in our minds—I guess we can stand the fact that some may think it peculiar for a man to have a small place of honor on the mantel over the fireplace for a Colorado pinecone or a rusty colored stone of no value, obviously, except for the one who brought it home.

The threads we use to find our way back through the day-to-day maze to where we were once close to the softness of contentment can come in very strange shapes indeed.

FOR BETTER OR WORSE

There are certain standards by which we all judge the joys of a hunting trip. One is the choice of a field partner. Yours and mine may well differ, but we are both specific about our likes and dislikes in the preference of a pal.

Needless to say, we like people who agree with or complement us in temperament and ability. (In my case it's a good thing that I don't mind gunning with better shots—simply because there are so many of them compared to the likes of me.) And to break this down a bit into specific details, I'd choose a man who wore a 46 gunning coat and always had rainwear, shot a 12-gauge gun, and had no strong objections to a glass or two of bourbon in the evening.

Now that's a pretty broad brush to which we could add a touch here and there, but not any of those statistics are by any means mandatory. As a matter of fact, I usually end up hunting with a guy who is barely a 38 chest, prefers a 20-bore shotgun, always forgets his parka, and is partial to rum. So much for externals; that's how they usually work out anyway. (Rita Hayworth's several husbands didn't include me or any of the guys I knew in the army, but we all had her picture tacked up as a constant reminder of what a pretty nifty woman looked like.)

What's really important on a gunning trip anyway—aside from the right guys to share it with—is the small talk in the camp; few things so fill me with that soft feeling of warm satisfaction as an evening spent discussing choke boring, shot sizes, drams equivalent, and the pros and cons of different gauges and actions in shotguns. This chitchat about the little things is equally divided into hearsay, rumor, opinion, guesswork—and now and then, if you're very alert, you might hear a fact or so fall into place.

I've noticed in the last few years as I've visited various duck clubs around the country that in any given duck club most of the members tend to use the same type of shotgun. Why? Is it that the talk has gone on so long that like a jury verdict one has been pronounced most fit and the members, to avoid breaking an unwritten law, have concurred? Did one man, one day, suddenly appear with a certain gun and begin wiping everybody's eye? Or is it just that in the interest of harmony such a thing evolved?

I remember a duck club down along the Maryland-Virginia shore where I shot some years ago. I arrived shortly after the members had gotten in from the evening flight, and they were all sitting around doing the necessary cleaning that a gun needs after a day on the salt marshes. Every single gun I saw was a Model 12 Winchester. And some men had two or three in the camp. Luckily, one of the duck guns I had in the car was an old three-inch magnum Model 12. So, when I went out and put it in the gun rack, half of my acceptance as a duck hunter with at least a little smarts was already established.

We still enjoyed our discussion of choke boring, shot sizes, and drams equivalent after dinner that night—but all within the confines of the basic Model 12.

But I've also walked into "over-and-under" duck clubs with an automatic, and into "automatic" duck clubs with a side-by-side. My mother didn't raise her boy to be a winner every time.

In the upland-bird crowd, the serious discussions that center around improved cylinder or modified, 6s or 8s, tend to be a little short in time compared to the opinions (expert and otherwise) strongly held on dogs: dogs in general as well as dogs in particular.

You'll notice one thing, however, about these dog arguments—and I swear it happens about 100 percent of the time. The best dog anyone ever saw, owned, or gunned over—the genuine nonpareil, the dog that would do it all and no questions asked, be it setter or pointer or what-have-you—is *never there in the area at this time!* This is as basic a law to bird dog conversation as the number of fish caught and released is to trout talk.

When the words get warm and the white-haired retired judge who hasn't raised his voice in years is now on his feet, locked into an imitation of a point that will have him bedridden in the morning, the perfect dog being exaggerated about is either dead or 2,000 miles away or both. Of course, everyone knows this and each, in his turn, is permitted to go on point or act out the scene of his choice, in the sure knowledge that he will never be asked to produce the sainted beast in the flesh.

I trust I don't leave the impression that I'm any different from anyone else when it comes to heated or softly persuasive speeches about anything to do with shotguns—again knowledge taking second place to opinion.

Nor can I plead anything but guilty if you ask me if I've ever gone on point (rather gracefully, I might add—from plenty of practice) or stood rigid as a granite carving to convey the staunchness of a favorite retriever.

But neither my opinions nor my convictions have ever carried the floor, since I am rather well known for spoiling both my dogs and the few opportunities I ever have at easy crossing shots. But I still cheerfully and adamantly tell the owners of champions the right and proper way to train retrievers and pointing dogs. And I have been known to give advice on technique and stance to trapshooters who would be delighted to spot me ten birds in 100.

Like everyone else, I live in that more perfect world of what-might-be; not possessing the talent (or the perfect shotgun) to be ever considered "decent," I gleefully recount the days that I rose to "average," and allude to days of sure and skillful shots that took place when no one else was there.

But all this only in hunting camps—where a man is among his own kind of special friends and where we extend each other privileges and considerations usually reserved for meetings between diplomats, or couples the first week they're engaged.

A hunting camp is one of the few places left to us where we can dream of a near-perfect tomorrow. Where the harsh realities of lost riches and faded glories can be forgotten and the dreams of what might be come down to a delightful day with not too much wind, a crisp morning silvered with frost, and find us—at long last—with the right gun, shells, dogs, and friends who will be pleased to forever remember the day we "did it all."

BOTTOMS UP!

I have read that John Woods, chief of the Fisheries Division of Florida, had discovered that bourbon obscures fish-frightening human odor. I don't know Mr. Woods personally, but I do know several fairly well-thought-of scientists, and while they might admire this "discovery" they would assuredly question his methods. His laboratory technique and the consequences are what capture my imagination.

Why bourbon? Or why only bourbon? Did Mr. Woods similarly try blended Scotch whiskey, rye, wine, beer, brandy, and gin? What about that old bass-fishing standby, corn liquor? How about applejack? Hard cider? And now, what kind of bourbon? Sour mash? Straight whiskies, blended bourbon, Kentucky bourbon, Tennessee bourbon, or Virginia bourbon?

I further must assume that Mr. Woods, though he may know

Florida bass fishing down to its common fractions, does not know
Florida bass fishermen. I am fortunate enough to know several, and
telling them that bourbon makes bass feel secure in their presence is
like telling them that you just caught two 15-pound fish on a plug.
Whereupon fishermen would endanger your life if you didn't tell
them what make plug, what size, what retrieve, what color, and
so on.

Every Florida bass fisherman (let's just say every bass fisherman and not single out Florida) has several hundred lures—that's
just types, I'm not counting color and size variations. Nor am I
adding plastic worms, pork rinds, flies, popping bugs, jigs, and live
bait rigs. I want to be conservative and believable. You go on and
tell a bass fisherman that using bourbon will help him catch more
bass, and you'd better either complete the sentence you started or
stand back.

I'm afraid that in the short piece I read, Mr. Woods further
neglected to say how this bourbon was to be used by the bass fisherman. I can guess how most bass fishermen would interpret this, but
I don't think that's how Mr. Woods meant it to be taken: although
I see no harm in it, used judiciously.

Using the same logic he used in plowing his daughter's dowry
into bass boats, motors (gas and electric), fish-finders, electronic
thermometers, lord knows how many spinning rods, casting rods,
worm rods, fly rods, and matching reels, along with 24,000 miles of
various kinds of lines, leaders, and not counting swivels, snaps, sink-
ers, and so on, what drastic steps is the average bass fisherman
going to take regarding bourbon? The mind reels, if you will
permit.

Did Mr. Woods try his secret bourbon method on trout or
catfish? These fishermen have a constitutional right to know. Or is
the work in progress? If that's so, then perhaps we should all pitch
in and shorten the research time. I, for one, am perfectly willing to
carry a small flagon of Scotch whiskey in my trout waders, and I'm
reasonably sure that if I asked similarly scientific-minded fishermen
that I know to do likewise, they would, like little soldiers, to a man,
do likewise.

I personally find drinking bourbon or Scotch, or whatever, less tiring to my eyes than tying No. 18 bivisibles in various shades, and would substitute one for the other occupation like a shot. (Should the type of whiskey turn out to be a greater factor in successful fishing than patterns and sizes and presentations, I would invest in a fishing tackle company or a distillery, or both.)

I think we'd all like to know more about this. What about smallmouth bass? Bream? Yellow perch, walleyes, shad? Are we close to needing less than 1,000 casts per muskie if we dip a Dardevle in Wild Turkey? Will gin be outlawed for Atlantic salmon along with the weighted fly? Will fish become "lure shy" if a lake is bombarded with bourboned plugs and refuse all but the rarest blends? Will white wine work better on clear days and red on cloudy days?

If this is the long-sought secret, what will happen to fishing writers who, by now, are unable to do an honest day's work? Will they devote their lives to research in this new field? Will tackle box manufacturers start building portable bars? Will the hollow glass rod now serve a new function? Will plugs be made in 86-proof and 100-proof sizes?

We'll have to revise all the old jokes like "we planned to fish for a week but we ran out of whiskey and had to come home in three days." Will this create another era of bootleg stuff? Will all the guys who write on new patterns of flies and new lures and so on start experimenting with yeast, sugar, and grain? Will the whiskey sour replace the muddler minnow? I don't really know how fish react to bourbon, personally, but I do know how a lot of fishermen react to it. And if fishermen and fish are as alike as a lot of people think—I know a lot of lakes I'm not going to fish on a summer Saturday night.

There's an old saying that goes "When the fisherman feels good, so do the fish." I once believed this had its basis on barometric pressures. Now I'm not sure. Maybe someone stumbled over the whole fish and whiskey idea some time ago.

Sometimes man's brightest ideas are out of phase with the essential character of man as a whole. Alfred Nobel invented dynamite as an aid to society and never dreamed it would be used in heavy weapons and bombs. Men first split the atom to find a source of cheap power to replace oil and coal. When Dom Perignon discovered champagne he said, "I am drinking stars." He had no idea it would be used at weddings.

What will be the ultimate outcome of Mr. Woods' discovery? I don't know, I'm a bit too cynical to scoff right yet. Some men take new ideas with a grain of salt. I'll take this one with a dash of bitters.

MORE BLESSED TO RECEIVE

Now that the cold breath of Christmas is being felt by laggard shoppers, it's time I did something to help out the many wives who are thinking about something suitable for The Old Trapper. In better days, she could just call his tailor and order a new tweed shooting coat, or his bespoke gunsmith for a sidelock 10-bore intended for pass shooting.

But since the economy has been giving us a right and a left, and craftsmanship is a word relegated to the dictionary for the most part, we are all forced to make do with items that are often less deep than our sentiment.

Since men will continue to give their wives useful things women really want—bird pluckers, shotshell reloaders, taxidermy kits, checkering tools, and fly-tying material—we need not be overly concerned with what endears us to our fair ladies.

But selecting the proper present for the Mr. involves a lot of problems. First, it's hard for many a woman to really be sure that her man doesn't already have the item in her mind. As shameless as it is, I do, in fact, know men who are not entirely candid with their wives about certain items—take shotguns and fly rods, for example. The very prudent wife should examine the attic for loose floor-boards that may very well conceal a cache of a Webley & Scott, two Perazzis, and a Pigeon Grade Model 12. Leonard and Orvis rods can, I am told, be easily hidden in a false section of cellar piping or slid into the interior of many standing lamps. (If I want to hide something from my wife, I merely put it in the closet that holds mops and the vacuum cleaner—an area as frequently visited as the Babuyan Islands.)

These items are, strangely enough, often not in the resident premises at all, in order to prevent the lady from sneering at the small number or low quality of her husband's little pleasures. (A local hunting and fishing clubhouse burned last summer, and when the paper printed the number of fly-rod and shotgun remains sifted out of the ashes—and, incredibly, their estimated value—several of my friends were suddenly summoned out of town on most impor-tant business trips.)

About now, the very observant wife (are there any other kind?) has noticed that certain catalog or magazine pages have turned-down corners. Sizes, gauges, lengths, etc., are likely to be noted or circled. Any of these showing up at Christmas will no doubt be found welcome. But the really grateful wife, although not overlooking these trifles, should go farther afield, keeping her at-tention keyed for subtle hints from the Lord and Master.

Should she notice the L & M idly poking at his waders with an ice pick, she knows that he is either in need of a new ice pick or a new pair of waders. Is he spending less than a complete weekend with his buddies in the field and at the gun club? The perceptive wife knows that a man who voluntarily spends time puttering around the house or chatting with his children is not normal. Is he cleaning his trap gun two or three times a week? Does he sit watch-ing television with his duck gun handy? Is he eating supper on Thursdays and Fridays with his gunning jacket on? If not, you ought to be calling the gunsmith . . . obviously there's a new shot-gun he needs desperately and doesn't have.

It's probably all right for a bride, in her innocence, to offer Mr. Right a case of high-brass 6s as a token of her esteem, but for the man who has been in the traces for over a decade—well, he sim-ply deserves more.

Common, but very gratefully received, gifts are a week of salmon fishing in Scotland, a high-country elk hunt—complete with a new 7mm Remington—or a goose blind for a few days on Mary-land's Eastern Shore.

If he's still got that errant poet in his eyes you used to enjoy so much, he'd find room for an original Hagerbaumer, Scott, Rene-son, Abbott, Maas, or a collection of Frosts. (If he already has some or all of these, he'd very likely enjoy more.)

If you've gotten the idea by now that I'm trying to say that most men are easy to please, you're right. Although we all know that it isn't the gift, but the giving, that counts, the average man is very flattered to know that his wife has enough appreciation for him to have memorized his stock measurements, his preference in fly-rod actions, as well as his trap and skeet averages.

Don't be put off by the possibility of spending too much, or being too frequent with remembrances throughout the year. Sev-eral dozen flies along about March take the chill from late winter as well as a new down duck-hunting parka will warm up a dreary No-vember. And luckily, for the ever-caring women, new products are always coming along at just the right time.

I'm sure your household diary notes what extra barrels are lacking for the shotguns, as well as when the double-tapered fly lines should be reversed, the outboard overhauled, the kennel bed-ding changed, and the important opening days. But if you are in the habit of making little entries about what your husband needs—try and keep it from his prying eyes. I happened to see the word RENO written in Marcia's calendar and I'm sure it stands for *R*eels, *E*dgeworth, *N*umber 2 shot, *O*pening day. I pretended I didn't see it because I don't want to spoil her little surprises.

SMALL MOMENTS

When I came off the stream, one of the other men in the camp was busily making notes in a small ledger. He was still at it after I had shucked off my waders, and I asked him if I could make him a drink while I was getting one for myself. He nodded, still obviously following some private vein of thought, when I held up the bourbon bottle, and when I had finished pouring I set his glass down on the table and lit my pipe.

"I'm keepin' a diary," he said. "Sort of basically a fishing log, but a little more than that."

I said I thought that was a good idea and went on about how often I wanted to remember a particular fly I'd used under certain conditions but how, with the passing of even a little time, I tended to forget. He was up poking at the fire while I chattered on about catching my first Atlantic salmon on a General Practitioner, and when he turned back to his chair he suddenly interrupted me and said ". . . no, that's really not what I meant." I waited for him to go on and he remained quiet for so long I guessed that he had said all he wanted and our conversation was over. But I was mistaken.

"My father was a fairly well-to-do man," he said, rather more or less as if he were just thinking out loud rather than talking to me. "He had the means and the time to fish virtually all the well-known water you can name—all over the United States, Canada, and most of England, Scotland, and Ireland. I don't think he ever went to Europe. I was kept in private schools and then off to summer camp until I was fifteen—that was the year he was killed in an accident. His car skidded off the road, turned over, and rolled into the river. I imagine he drowned, but to this day I'm not sure." He waved his drink toward the corner of the cabin and said, "That was his favorite trout rod. It's a Leonard. He liked the little Leonards for trout, but his big salmon rods were made by Payne. And I really don't know a great deal more about him than that."

I got up and took his glass and made us another bourbon and water. When I came back, he had pulled his chair closer to the fire, facing it rather than me. I watched the light from the fire play on his face as he continued.

"That summer, when I was fifteen, was when I began fishing myself. I was tired of camps; I had the money; my mother was glad to see me go—so I went.

"I think I got started fishing to build in my own mind a feeling about a man who cared more about being more or less alone than he cared about being with his family. That is, my mother and myself. I know now why he and she didn't get along—it's not important— just one of those things. But I sort of felt that that summer was the one when he would have started taking me along. So I went myself—always imagining what it would have been like had he been with me."

I put another small log on the fire and sat back down.

"I began keeping a diary then," he continued "in a way for the father I had never known. At first it was your ordinary day's-end entries . . . what the water was like, the weather, the rods and flies I used—all the common observations. But gradually I felt that it was important to do more than that, so I began to write to myself. It was a lonely life in a way, casual friendships made here and there—promises to meet later in the city that were never kept—or really meant to be. I wanted to put down in words who I was. To the casual observer I'm sure I came off as a rather shallow person, wrapped in fishing during the day and reading alone in the evening."

A loon began calling from somewhere off on the lake and he got up and went outside to listen. I intended not to follow, but he stood in the door holding it open in invitation and so I tagged along. We watched as the early evening moonlight buttered the surface of the water.

"That's the sort of thing I write about," he said, sweeping his hand toward the lake, the haunting loon, and the singular brilliance of the evening star.

"You have to know how you feel about things like that to know who you are. At first I was only interested in catching the most and the biggest fish. But that's all I saw—some sort of measured success. Like most young men, I saw too much of everything to see anything. Another interest I enjoyed was birds. I kept a list of those. And it was, oddly enough, one of the most common sights we all see that changed the way I began thinking. It was a single red-winged blackbird, perched on a water reed. One of those long-stalked rushes, like cattails. The bird was sitting on the upper third of the reed, swinging up and down. I stopped fishing and watched this single bird. I don't know how long it had been sitting there, but it began to occur to me that this bird was having a marvelous time. I could *feel* it. I could sense the pleasure of this simple creature and began feeling a great deal of enjoyment myself—I was sharing its delight at being alive and clever enough to have created a swing out of what a moment or so before had only been a reed.

"Where there had been nothing—the bird had created something. That was very impressive to me. Not a great thought perhaps, a far cry from a revelation or philosophical insight, but the whole thing gave me a great deal of satisfaction."

"I've seen the same thing myself many times," I said, "but what you saw and felt never occurred to me."

"You don't think the whole thing is silly?" he asked.

"Not at all," I told him.

"Well," he said, "that's the sort of thing I'm writing down in my ledger. A small and modest chronicle of things that make my days worth remembering—at least to me. Someday someone, maybe a son of mine, will read these things and know that I could be made happy by the smallest of moments. And that the things I came fishing to find turned out not to be fish. And that I found them."

He turned and went inside, leaving me alone in the softness of the near-night, thinking about a lot of strange things I hadn't thought about for a long time and hoping that I might—right then—see a red-winged blackbird settle on a reed and begin to swing itself. It didn't happen, but then, things like that never do.

THE KID WHO TRAVELS WITH ME

I was reading the opinion of one of our leading economists the other day and he said that his feelings about the future ranged back and forth between misery and despair.

Well, since I've never heard a cheerful economist—I doubt if there is one—I wasn't too troubled. My personal savings run to shotguns, fly rods, duck boats, outdoor books, and some good prints. I figure if you can shoot it, fish with it, or float around in it, you're solvent. I want my bank account to read about the same when I leave this world as it did when I came into it: $00.00. My wife thinks I may hit that figure prematurely, or even quicker than that, if I don't learn a little better pace. Well, she's part economist by nature, so I tend to avoid pessimistic discussions with her.

The way I like to look at it is simpler, obvious, and provable. Take fly rods. They've about doubled in price while I was waiting for things to level off a little. My mistake. Shotguns? If I had followed my instincts I'd be well set—but I couldn't convince the Chairman. Now and then I remind her about the Model 21 Winchesters I could have (and should have, and would have, except for being broke) picked up for $300 or so, the Westley Richards Best Grade for $700, or the $1,200 Purdey. All, alas, have gone to more solvent fellows—and I wish them all well.

Other folks I know are in the shuffle between misery and despair about time, or lack of it. They never seem to get away—they're too busy making a lot of money for stuff they can't afford anyway. And if you don't have the time to use it, what good is it? A man has to stop every so often and say to himself: "Wait just a minute—where are you running off to, and why?" And if he's got any sense, he ought to be honest a few times before his relatives wheel him off out of the way.

It's smart of you to keep your outgo a little less than what's coming in, I agree to that. But I've decided I've passed too many rising trout simply by being too busy. I've driven by too many birdy covers on the way to work and have seen Saturday turn up pouring rain—all my life; up until now.

I don't really regret not ever having a best-grade gun or the ultimate trout rod, but I do talk to myself now and then about the times when I should have gone out and used what I have—but didn't. As I look back, I don't think it would have made too much difference in the long run if I had—it wouldn't with most of us, except that it might have diminished our silly attitude of self-importance; small loss that, at best. We ought to stop a minute and take a long look ahead—as far as we're able. Are we waiting too long to do the things we work so hard for? Will they all be there when the day comes that we can say, "I'm ready now!"?

Well, no one has given us a written guarantee, that I know for sure. I'm pretty strong on the theory that the future is tomorrow—and if I can, I'll go fishing, or fool with my dog, or do something else that pleasures me and offers me something sweet to remember.

There's another side to each one of us—a part of our being that we know well enough but keep more or less secret from everyone else. The one I live with is still a kid, barefoot and straw-hatted in summer; a kid who always knew where the best perch holes were, when the bass were off the nests, where the owls had their roost, and which brush piles were most likely to hold rabbits. He was a kid who found wonder and excitement almost beyond comprehension in the trying-out of a new plug, or getting fitted for a new pair of hip boots. He's basically a good and simple boy—a tendency to day-dream notwithstanding. And I think the time has come to really try and keep the promises I made to him too many years ago; to give the farm-boy wishes some chance of coming true. There were dreams of serpentining northern rivers to be covered by canoe, and of high-country pack trips for rocking-chair muleys and park-statue elk. And there were visions of blue-water marlin, Florida bass, and Montana trout; New Brunswick woodcock, Michigan grouse, and Texas quail; flights of pintails and an anxious Lab; flocks of honkers sliding down blindward on the notes of a goose call.

Although the boy is ageless, the man he lives inside of feels the winter coming on; he believes that, in a certain way, a hope worked for is a debt that should be paid. Some of them already have been—but by no means all. It's a long list, and I only wish we'd started at it somewhat sooner.

Dreams have a way of begetting dreams, however, and the promises kept lead to promises to come. The rivers turn out to be endless, and the singing of the evening coveys from somewhere we have yet to go will keep us coming back—and will stay the touch of time from the other side of us that keeps us company when an out-sider, wrongly, thinks we are alone.

Time is not really money, as the more industrious of our world would have us follow as a creed. You can't put it away, not a single hour, and come back and use it when the situation seems more right. My most important savings have been memories of the things I did, sometimes with tortured conscience, when there were more "worthwhile" occupations that more dutiful men than I would have tended. But somehow the regrets have faded while the pleasure stays with me even now.

I'm learning not to feel guilty, and it isn't all that easy, about going fishing on Tuesday or spending a Thursday in a duck blind. But it helps a lot to know that both I and the kid that travels with me prefer our savings to be the silver of a summer brook and the gold of a late-autumn bird cover.

STARTING THEM OUT

It used to be, in somewhat better times, that when one of the chips off the old block got to be gunning age, somebody handed him one of the old pieces that sat in the kitchen closet by the stove, or better yet, a once-in-a-lifetime trip was made to hardware stores and the vast array of smoothbores was trundled out and long discussions about kick and gauge and weight and choke boring deliciously preceded the spending of a hard-farmed 40 or 50 dollars.

The recipient of such a gun was usually in the neighborhood of 10 to 12 years old, size being more important than calendar. They used to say that you had to have enough heft to handle a team without having to put rocks in your britches.

And by this time the would-be gunner had put in many, many hours trudging after the men in the family as they covered the partridge covers, or sitting in a blind in the role of a very quiet observer, toter of supplies, carrier of game, and a lookout after the dogs. He had seen how it was done. He had spent countless evenings in front of the kitchen stove listening to the tales, long, tall, and otherwise, about how it should be done. He more than likely had long run his own trapline so he was somewhat of a naturalist. He knew where to look for game and how to walk through the woods. He was careful of manly things like axes, knives, and guns. Not only because they were expensive, but because they were tools that had to be cared for if they were to be depended on. He had been allowed to heft and clean guns for nearly as long as he could remember. Finally owning his own was just the last step in a coming of age. He had passed all the tests; he could be trusted.

Today, for the most part, it isn't done that way. More often than not a youngster hasn't had the time or the opportunity to garner the experience, learn the subtleties and the self-confidence and the self-discipline to just pick up his first gun and step out with Old Jack snuffling along at his side.

Teaching a beginner to shoot today has, in my opinion, become a quite complicated affair. In fact, the shooting itself is about the last part of teaching gun handling in the field. I'm talking here of shotgunning—and youngsters. I take great care to avoid the beginning adult. He thinks he knows too much, or is convinced that by being an American he was born with the God-given ability to handle a gun. I'm scared to death of the man, or child, who isn't scared of a gun.

One instructive technique I know of began with the teacher taking his pupil out to the field and at close range blowing a pumpkin to bits with a 12-gauge, just as a way of impressing the student of the awesome destructive power of a shotgun. Not the world's worst idea, since I know of very few gunners who haven't, at one time or another, shot when they didn't want to, or have had a gun go off by "accident."

TEACHING

I like to teach the way I learned. Partly because I'm old-fashioned and partly because I believe in it. The first step (really steps) is simply to have the child carry an empty gun in the field with you for several outings. And I have several reasons for this. One is that I believe there is only one way to carry a gun muzzle—and that is to always have it pointed in the air and away from your gunning partner and away from the dog and away from your foot. Away from *anything.* By carrying, the student learns several other things instinctively. Gun balance—where it's most comfortable to hold a gun. He or she learns the "feel" of a gun; where it rests most lightly and yet can come quickly to hand. I also insist that the empty gun be kept handy in the house and handled at every opportunity—for a few minutes at a time. This reinforces the above lessons and goes further into creating a subconscious muscle knowledge of gun handling. A golfer who spends the winter carrying a golf club around the house may feel slightly silly, but it will definitely build in "hand memory" for the feel and balance of a club. Guns are no different. A shooter has to learn to handle his firearm and there are no shortcuts. One of the many mistakes most of us make in teaching a youngster to shoot is to teach him *how* before we teach him *when* and *why*. In today's aggressive and growing sentiments against hunting it is more important than ever to create in a youngster a feeling of the ethics, the traditions, and a knowledge of where man has been as a hunter and where he hopes to go.

Most of this comes about naturally with time and exposure. You have a house with sporting magazines, books, more than likely a print or two of ducks, dogs on point, and the casual goings on that are part of the hunting style. The chatting between friends, the walks with the dogs on training sessions. The observance of the life cycle of local game. If you're lucky enough to have a local gun club that can show a movie once in a while, make it a family or youngster night for one of the many films that are offered for the asking from many outdoors-oriented companies.

Take the kids along to the trap and skeet outings. Take them along when you sight in a rifle—and make them part of it, even without allowing them to shoot if they're not ready. Let them paste targets, pick up empties—whatever, but get them involved.

A young boy or girl who only knows how to pick up a 20-bore and break a few targets or grass a ringneck or quail might very well know virtually nothing about the sport of hunting. I know a young boy who's shot three white-tailed deer with about as much interest and emotion (maybe less) as if they'd been so many tin cans at a rifle range. He isn't what I want along as a hunting companion, now or ever. I want a young boy or girl that asks the silly questions—and if I don't know the answers I'll say so, and then find out. I like kids that are interested in pine siskins, jack-in-the-pulpits, buck rubbings, possum tracks, cirrus clouds, the North Star, birch bark, and all the other magnificent and insignificant question marks that punctuate a day in the woods. First we ought to create the interest in hunting; then the hunter will most likely create himself.

My own daughters know how to care for the dogs as well as I can, and can identify a good many more wild birds and at least as many wild plants, flowers, and trees. They know how to pluck a bird and scale a fish. Not only as a curious skill, but because it's a practical need in our house. The outdoors is part of our life—not merely a dress-up occasional hobby. I hate seeing a youngster shoot a quail and then be gingerly fastidious about picking it up and gutting it. I dislike even more a parent who lets him get away with it—or worse, acts that way himself.

Before a young sprout gets a gun he ought to know that a good part of gunning is messy. It's bloody. It often involves wounded game. It always involves guts, defeathering, and skinning. If he can't take that—and he should long have had his share before he pops one cap—he isn't a hunter. He has to know wet feet, thorns, briars, and being hot, tired, and those days when everything that can go wrong does. When he can bring a little understanding to the side of hunting not featured in gun catalogs and not often talked about at the dinner table, then he's ready.

I'm often asked about the beginner's shotgun. No, I'm more often told that so-and-so is getting his or her first gun—a .410. And I know that the beginner is in for trouble. Alex Kerr and a few others can hit targets and game with a .410 shotgun, but few others can. I can't, and I'm not the world's worst shot. I believe that the little guns—the .410 and even the 28—belong only on the skeet field or in the hands of a top-flight shot who knows what the small bores can't do—and doesn't try.

Let's assume that the first gun is a 20-gauge. And let's put the light load in it: 2¼ drams equivalent and 7/8 ounce of shot. And let's start with a moving target—a clay bird thrown from a hand trap.

I have a lot of trouble teaching most youngsters how to shoot because I just can't see what they see over a gun barrel. What I do is to teach them to stand correctly, the right place to put the gun in the pocket of their shoulder, and the position of the hands. I also try to exhibit gun safety as much or more than I talk about it in order not to turn into a middle-aged bore. But I make sure that my lessons are listened to. And I make sure that *they do it*—as well as myself. And the minute I see their attention span or interest lag, or overdiscouragement set in—the lesson stops, just as it would if I were training a puppy.

We all ought to remember, even though we haven't talked too much to the pupil about it, that even a 20 kicks and makes more noise than they're used to. I take for granted that the first dozen shots or so are done with both eyes firmly shut. (I'm sure mine were—and judging by some of my shooting, I'm sure they still are every once in a while.)

My basic theory is plenty of shells and clay targets—and patience. If you can really see the shot path that's behind or over the target, fine. But look more closely at stopping the gun muzzle, raising the head or standing wrong—which is usually leaning over too far backwards, especially in girls. And don't forget that the straightaway target is not nearly as easy as it looks to the beginner (or the expert, for that matter) so put a little angle on it so that the picture of lead can take some form.

COMMON SENSE

Please don't expect too much. And please don't forget that the little guy you're trying to teach is trying much harder to please you, and do it well. If you have access to a skeet range, I know of no way better to show a youngster than a few shots at low house seven, and then high seven. Then move between low six and seven and get a little angle practice. If a youngster can hit these angles, he is pretty well started out for field gunning—as long as he knows that missing or hitting isn't really that important—now or ever.

I like to teach the way I train dogs, with a very positive approach. Praise and discussion over the things done right and well and little or no discussion over the mistakes—with the exception of carelessness. Watching good shots at trap or skeet is very helpful to the observant student, if you can point out why targets are broken: proper stance, good gun position, strong follow-through. Youngsters like to imitate. If you've got a good shot who doesn't mind coaching your kids, let him go ahead. Most children will listen to almost anyone rather than their parents anyway.

I don't wholly agree with the two-eyes-are-better-than-one theory. I really do, but not necessarily for the starter. It seems instinctive to want to point and aim a shotgun as you would sight a rifle. If they can break targets with one eye shut—fine. A little later you can get them to try it with both eyes open, as you should. But, most important, you have to keep in mind the whole purpose of hunting and shooting instruction and exposure. It's not to fill up another license and bag limit. It's to create in someone else the same feeling you and your friends have about the guns and the game and the dogs and the rest.

Simply stated, a gun is a key to the rest of it. It unlocks the doors to many paths. Guns have created, in their own way, my most enriching friendships. A knowledge of fine people that shared a common bond with me because of shooting and the other things that go with it. A knowledge of dogs—and the shared things that go with living with them. A knowledge of quiet. A knowledge of small sounds and the sometime furies that we enjoy most by being in their midst.

Shooting *itself* is probably the least of it—but only the real gunner understands that. I know it's probably bad taste to quote yourself, or at least impolite—but be that as it may. Sometime ago I wrote a small essay about why I intended to give my girls their own guns when the proper time came along; I felt that since my attitude about the outdoors was the most of my worldly legacy, I ought to write something that explained how I felt about it. In slightly different words I said, "As long as there is such a thing as a wild goose, I leave you the meaning of *freedom*. As long as there is such a thing as a hunting dog, I leave you the meaning of *loyalty*. As long as there is such a thing as having your own gun and a place to walk free with it, I leave you the feeling of *responsibility*. This is part of what I give you when I give you your first gun."

MY RESPECTS TO MR. BOB

I'd like for you to wander around with me while I mess with quail. I know it's kind of a funny way to put it, but quail days seem to be filled with a soft and very special music. The slow melody of a Southern afternoon itself, with Red or Billy Joe singing out "Slow there, Sally . . . Rip—stay put" . . . and, like a crackling brown burst of flame, the birds arise and flare, then drift like smoke back into the dark and deep and green.

If you know me, you know I'm a Yankee-born. But if you know me very well, you know I like the liquid sound of saying that a lot of Alabama-Georgia folk could call me kin. So, although it sounds a little strange, I feel pretty much at home, down South, and gunning quail.

No picture that I carry in my mind is more vivid than remembering my first-time, deep-Southern shoot and a pair of pointers, one lemon-ticked and the other with peanut-butter-colored spots, standing spine-high in broom grass between the shafts of shadow thrown by spindly pines. I felt strange and somewhat rude as I walked in behind the point and honor—I was a man walking into what was so much like a famous painting that I almost had to laugh.

But, if you're lucky, that's what a lot of quail hunting is—a series of lovely paintings that we walk into and out of all day long. If you sketched me in, you'd better have a trembling brush. Quail always have—and I'm afraid always will—scared the hell out of me. But I don't mind—after all, that's kind of why I'm there.

Anyone who's messed with quail has messed with some mighty strange dogs. Pointers and setters so pretty you could cry at the perfection of line that shapes their gallant heads, and scruffy droppers, or of even less visual lineage, with so many of the pretty ones worthless and so many of the others simply "not for sale."

I remember gunning in North Carolina, years ago, over a sort of plum-colored little dog that might have been setter and springer and pointer—and a little something else thrown in just for luck—but to the young man who owned her she was simply his bird dog. Even he didn't say she was anything else but "his dog." But he was a quail hunter, and as they say, "Papers don't pin down coveys." And that Queenie could do. It might be very fair to describe her as as good as she was homely. She did what she was supposed to do and expected to do, with no fanfare, no praise, no petting—almost no notice.

I was tempted once to mention that Queenie had done a really fine piece of work on a very touchy covey, but then, with a little thought for once, thought better of it and kept my mouth shut. It would have meant no more to the man who owned her than if I'd sat watching him plow half a field and then had gone over and praised his tractor.

Queenie. Have you ever hunted a season without working behind a dog called Queen? Can't be done. Nor can you miss a Jack, Lady, Jill, or Buck. And you're going to hunt those Jills and Bucks around the schoolhouse covey, the churchyard covey, and the cabin covey. I sometimes suspect that there are more "churchyard coveys" in Georgia than there ever were churchyards, but we all know that there are some things you don't get talking about, especially if you're a Yankee: Gettysburg, Baptists, and what the lemony-colored stuff is in the Mason jar. The side-traditions of quail hunting are a lot more than shotguns, dog flesh, and cream gravy.

I like all the traditions of quail hunting. Especially the stories; the kind that, if they aren't true, they ought to be. I don't know when they all started, but I'd bet that the oldest one is about the dog that was lost and finally, after a week or so of looking around and advertising for him, he was just given up and forgotten—until two years later, back in the same area, they found the skeleton of a pointer, and when they looked around a little more, the skeletons of eight quail. Now you'll hear that before they pass the Mason jar around the second time. Then'll come the ones about Old Preacher; he could count and would tap his paw on the ground for you to let you know how many birds there were in the covey. And standing behind these dogs might be Leroy—he's the man who carried an old model 97 Winchester hammer pump and could put down five quail on a big rise nine times out of ten. I guess that Old Jesse ought to only have hunted with Leroy, because he's the dog that wouldn't hunt with you if you missed three times running—just go back and sulk scornfully under the wagon.

They say you can't profit as much by other people's mistakes as you can by your own, but mine are universal enough to be passed on. It ought to be basic that you brag neither about your shooting ability nor about your dog's superlative qualities—before they have been demonstrated. Looking down the throat of a jar may make you feel like Narcissus staring into the spring—but resist, my friend, for I have sat in that seat, and it can be mighty uncomfortable the next day. Let somebody else shoot over the first point of the day—it's a lot easier on the nerves the second time the covey bomb goes off. Try to say something nice about your host's dog—if you hardly see him all afternoon, mention that you like the way he covers ground. If you've stepped on him and stumbled over him every so often, note how close he works in a nice clear voice. But don't get carried away like one friend of mine who gushed and praised and came close to lyric verse over one dog every time he went on point and retrieved a bird, until finally the exasperated owner said "My God, man, that's what he's *s'posed* to do!" If you're lucky enough to have a good day behind your gun, give that the soft pedal; nothing was ever said truer than that the sun don't shine on the same dog's rear every day.

At the camp table there will be some green stuff that looks odd to the stranger. This is either collards or beet greens. Both very good. There's another green veg that tastes like library paste—that's okra. Most everything else is easily recognized—but a word of caution: You can find harder ways of starting a fight than to say the ham is too salty—that's the way it's done in some places, so just drink lots of water. Do not ever, unless you and your Daddy were born and raised in the county, touch one drop of the stuff in the jar filled with little red and green or yellow peppers; it's no worse than being kicked in the mouth by a mule, but no better either. Take my word for it—those peppers would raise a blister on a work glove . . . they're only there in case the local sheriff drops in and wants to feel mean all afternoon.

I consider myself sort of an authority on Southern cooking because I was raised on it. Everything is boiled or fried or both. Only biscuits, johnny cake, cornbread, and pies and cakes are baked. I could live, and have, on a diet composed in the main of cornbread, chitlins, and buttermilk. Grits and red-eye gravy is as good as anything that ever came out of France, as are ham hocks and black-eyed peas. Dixie cooking is like sour mash—when it's so-so it's still good, and when it's good it's ambrosia.

Sooner or later the good talk creeps in, and the men shuffle around and drag out the gun cases and barrels, and fore-ends are clicked into place. As much as I like the doubles, I know what a man can do with a pump gun. And I doubt if anything has brought down more birds than the fine-pointing, hump-backed Browning. But for much the same reasons that I'll sometimes gun wearing a necktie, I like the old side-by-sides. And if I were given a dream-come-true gun to haul up with me in the democrat wagon, I know just what I'd like; and, like a lot of good things, it's a victim of progress—or what they call old-fashioned. A real 16 would make me smile. And not too light—say about 6½ pounds, maybe a bit more. I've found out the hard way that light guns are sweet to carry, but as easy to stop in the swing as they are to start. Make it with 28-inch barrels so it would be smooth-flowing on crossing shots, and cylinder-bore in the first barrel and about 40 percent of choke in the second. It would have a straight-grip, English-style stock, a single trigger, and a splinter fore-end. I'd like it just a bit dressed up, the way I like to see a pretty girl. A gold disc with my initials in the stock and some classic floral etching on the receiver. I suppose I wouldn't do much better or worse with my dream 16 than I would with your 20 or 12, but I just happen to like it, for no better or worse reason than I like orange-ticked setters and liver-and-white pointers, old corduroy coats and soft felt hats. All put together, it's a rather shambling excuse for style—but it's me, for better or worse. But here we go. You with your favorite gun and me with mine, up behind a pair of dogs who have done their job and expect us to do ours.

My job seems to be to stand there and shake for a minute and then shoot just over one or two birds. At least on the first covey. Then I kind of calm down and scratch out the odd bird or so over the next few points.

I consider myself a pretty good duck shot, average or so on doves and grouse, but quail can do a number on me, more often than not. Now, I know how to gun quail as well as you do. You just remain calm, pick a bird out of the 23 that just unexpectedly exploded under your feet and headed low and fast over the 2½ yards that separated them from some pitch-black hole in the honeysuckle. Nothing to it. We've seen it done time and time again. Two shots, two trips for dogs, and on to the next covey. I won't bore you with a list of the things I can't do well, but getting applause from my compatriots on my behavior in such a situation is not a regular thing. I stand there and marvel, I stand there shocked, scared, bewildered, and stupefied. I watch a good part of the forest floor take to random wing and leave my safety on, change my mind six times, shoot twice into a solid mass of feathers, and watch them all disappear intact.

The first time or so the man handling the dogs comes over and shouts "Dead bird!" where there would be a dead bird if Annie Oakley were gunning. The dogs look at me as if they just saw me pick pennies out of the poor box—they know if and where something needs their attention, and I know they know. I tell old Red that I had a little trouble with the safety and let's move on to pick up the singles.

Now, I'm death on singles in any kind of open cover. Well, maybe not death exactly, but nobody has to look away all day and pretend they're not laughing. There are several things a quail can do that surprise me, a few things that amaze me, and one or two that render me as ineffective as a stone dog on a lawn. But, by and large, the odds are in my favor if I have to have birds for supper. A few quail are smarter than I am, but not all of them.

At least I've quit saying "Fly on with your heart shot out." I've quit staring at the empty and then putting it carefully in my pocket, remarking "I ought to send this one back to Remington." But I haven't quit smiling—I've just quit thinking that I ought to do better than I know how.

Anyway, since the average quail costs us about $30 a pound, not counting incidentals, travel, and excise tax, and the cook is having pork chops for dinner anyway, all I really have to worry about is staying on the good side of the dogs.

About the time of day when the sun sinks down to where it just pinks the scrub oaks and the owls start shooing you off, it's a natural instinct to swing toward the spot you like to save for last. One gunning friend called it his "sundown covey," and that says as much about it as has to be said. Yours may be by the trumpet vines and mine by what's left of a corncrib, but it always seems important to have this little evening rendezvous—to pause and give our best regards to Mr. Bob.

The music of the day comes to its sweetest end with that small whistle we have come to catch and carry with us in our ear and in our heart. With Old Jesse and Queenie, perked up and heading for the barn, at our heels and maybe a sliver of moon to silver the path, we might do well to stop once more, say we'd like to light our pipe—and hope that somewhere amidst the easy sounds of dusk we hear him one more time. Just to make sure that there will be something good waiting for us in our tomorrows.

AN IDLE DREAM

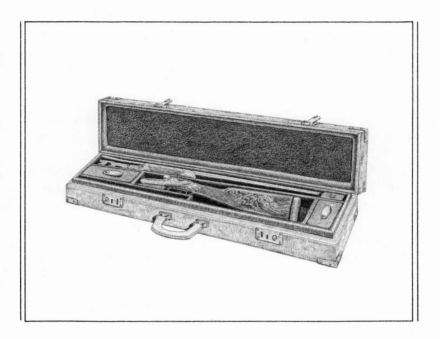

I see myself, in my idle dreaming hours, in an old red Buick convertible with the top down. I am wearing a faded corduroy cap that I heavily favored (now long lost), enjoying a big curved Dunhill pipe (also favored and long lost), with my bird dog sitting up on the front seat with me, grinning into the breeze as dogs often do.

This, to me, is a soft picture reflecting a sweeter time. I would have been headed for a bird cover that I know now is checkered with cheaply built houses.

I am looking for a time when a fine, or at least good, side-by-side cost less than a car. A time when you were allowed to go out wearing whatever seemed suitable and not a required minimum of plastic fluorescent orange.

A time when you could drink from a spring without fearing instant hepatitis or worse. A time when a lost dog would bring a friendly telephone call saying that Jeff was in a neighbor's kitchen eating corn bread, and I could come fetch him—instead of being sick with worry about dog thieves.

A time when a farmer whom I didn't happen to know would be pleased to have a chat, warn me about the pasture where the bull was kept, and more often than not insist on a cool glass of sweet (or better yet—hard) cider from a frog-sprinkled spring house . . . instead of being threatened with arrest for trespassing or treated with fearful suspicion.

A time when you could set up a fly rod and leave it by the car and expect to find it when you came back from gunning a morning cover.

I liked it better when my hunting license was a little green or orange pin that I fastened to my hat instead of a three-page legal document that I have to display pinned to my back like a prison number.

I deeply miss the afternoons when we could get together at the trap club and swap a gun, or take another one home to try out without being in violation of Lord knows how many state and federal laws threatening us with confiscation, massive fines, and jail.

I miss the excitement children had at being allowed to tag along to watch Bess work a cover and maybe take a shot or two to see how far along they were in growing up—when the fathers and mothers were trusted to teach them good gun manners instead of well-meaning strangers who put them through what's optimistically called a Hunter's Safety Course and give them a paper that makes them much more confident than they should be.

I don't like to have to sign half a dozen forms to buy a box of .22s. I resent being fingerprinted and forced to carry a permit that remarks on my sanity and questions my civil obedience.

Where did everything go wrong? What happened to us? Why did our society make us display ourselves as moronic, dangerous, destructive, and law-breaking? Our glowing plastic vests flapping with tags, our serial numbers duly registered with the national and local authorities, our morals questioned, and our intentions scrutinized?

I don't know. But I can't resign myself to being legally classified as an equal to a house thief, an armed robber, or a potential murderer. But that's the case, like it or not, before we can enjoy a round of trap or a sunrise from a duck blind.

My nongunning neighbors equate me with the disappearance of everything from the great auk to the passenger pigeon. They accuse me of being a factor in the diminution of the trumpeter, the osprey, and about everything else but the saber-toothed tiger and the mastodon. Television and popular magazines portray me as a blood-covered savage with instincts that would be demeaning to prehistoric man.

My children are abused in school, and my neighbors send the police over if I pattern a shotgun in the backyard or mess with a few clays and my hand trap.

My empty gun case in the room with the big fireplace mocks my reflection in the glass. And I stand there—looking at myself— and dream of the days you could drive through town with the top down, smoking your pipe and wearing your favorite old corduroy cap, your dog sitting grandly in the front seat. The neighbors all knew you were going bird hunting, and they would wave and wish you well. The gravel roads crossed and recrossed our brooks, threaded through our woodcock and partridge covers, and led us home again with a lovely song that added a sweetness to those little travels.

But, as many poets tell us, there are roads we may have traveled once that we can never take again.

THE ZERN

Having spent a good deal of the past summer traveling with my wife and my teen-age daughter, as well as a few journeys with one of my fellow writers who has three of everything in the sporting goods line, my scientific bent has led me to the invention or creation of a unit of encumbrance, which I call a ZERN—simply because it has a nice, scientific ring to it, like "erg" or "OHM."

A Zern is basically determined by utility (or better, nonutility) as well as mass and/or weight. For example: a Zern of fishing equipment would mean having four rods and a comparable number and variety of lures and tackle boxes, where a single rod and two or three plugs would be adequate. A serious trapshooter might arrive at a three-day shoot with two Zerns of stuff—or roughly four times what he could possibly be expected to need regardless of what might possibly happen—including natural disasters, Acts of God, and other such descriptions of the remote that we find in all our insurance policies.

A basic Zern is at least 50 percent more than necessary in number, at least 50 percent heavier to carry than it need be, and should take up at least 50 percent more room. A teen-age daughter can be counted on to leave for a trip of a week's duration with three Zerns of luggage, including stuffed animals, a clothes change for every half-hour, and emergency rations (potato chips, soda, cookies, etc.) sufficient to cross the Antarctic. Her mother takes an equal or larger amount, leaving the tour guide with a displaced vertebra from slinging the luggage into the van, and perhaps room for a half-Zern of his own stuff, which, of course, must include everyone else's fishing equipment, waders, vests, bug spray, etc., etc.

A Zern need not necessarily stand for tonnage, but merely to measure wretched excess. A big-game dude who is carrying a belt knife, a minihatchet, a Swiss Army knife, and one of those new fingertip-skinning devices might be said to be carrying a Zern of cutlery. (A lumpy tarpaulin once covered a pack of stuff on a horse that I happily discovered to be a Zern of whiskey and beer.)

I am not immune, either, to be typically honest about my rare shortcomings, as I own a near-Zern of hats, a full Zern of fly reels, and have every intention of harboring a Zern or two of trap guns.

Every great discovery like this one has in its background a moment of mystery that leads to a near-divine moment of revelation. One second, the thing is obscure, clouded in form, elusive in the mind—and then there it is . . . A TRUTH! It's clear as a bell—so obvious that one wonders why the moment of understanding has so long eluded the most inquiring minds of mankind. While it is not my intent to brag, I believe that the Zern will come to rank in utility to civilization somewhere above the Laws of Newton and below Dom Perignon's discovery of champagne. The semisciences like psychology, advertising, and stock-market analysis will come to find it part of their everyday usage, adding immeasurably to their free-form vocabulary of meaningless, indistinct, and fraudulent terminology.

The first seeds of this discovery, as I seem to remember, occurred on a canoe trip some years ago. The journey involved several portages, but the fishing was restricted to smallmouth bass. Accordingly, I carried a plug rod for a lake that was involved and a fly rod for the fast-water sections of the river. My lures and flies fitted neatly into one shirt pocket; my other duffle was easily carried in my canvas kit bag. The old, pat phrase "barest minimum" would describe my outfit perfectly. However, another member of the party, whose identity common decency forbids me to name, came to the canoe obscured by a forest of rods ("obscured," here, is a figure of speech; had he been less portly, it would have been most apt), and sweating under the burden of waders, boots, rain gear, and miscellaneous impedimenta that could have competed with a sporting-goods table at a flea market. It was at this moment, I am sure, that the idea was born, but thanks only to the years of my celebrated abstinence was it allowed to live and arrive here, now, and full-grown.

Marriage, of course, and the fact that I have two daughters, must take a major supporting role in my attentions (both physical and intellectual) to the study of excessive burdens in my everyday life. The pure poundage of my wife's luggage for a weekend trip would do credit to a farrier. Either of my daughters is capable of packing enough bathing suits to do justice to a Miss America contestant, with an accompanying wardrobe that might be the envy of an international film star. If there is ever an Olympic event in suitcase-lifting, I ought to at least make it to the semifinals.

The celebrated Dr. Johnson is credited with a definition of a gentlemen as one "who knew how to play the bagpipes but didn't." One could make a parallel of this with a sportsman who might have Zerns of equipment but didn't always carry it *all* around *all* the time.

There are certain habits that by their nature require near-Zerns of stuff: pipe smoking, duck hunting, photography, fly fishing, and often trapshooting. A half-Zern, commonly the amount a normal man can carry without making two trips, ought to suffice under the most extended circumstances; even involving a journey that, at its most extreme, would include both fly fishing and trapshooting. To subject a man who smoked a pipe, took pictures, and fly fished to one more activity per trip, would immediately be classified by the Civil Liberties Union as cruel and unusual punishment.

If my concept takes hold the way I foresee it will, then, as a public service, a list of precise definitions that might serve useful to most of us in our day-to-day carryings-on should be refined and formulated. You might shoot a Zern of shells practicing on right angles from Station Five, but you could not, properly, say you had a Zern of misses—although I'm afraid it might be used this way on occasion. You might be whimsical and say, after picking up a fellow goose hunter's lunch pail: "Boy, that's about a bottle of wine shy of a Zern!" You could drink a Zern of beer, but you could not have a Zern of a hangover. A Zern ought not be an abstract, but is properly involved with the physical, the tangible, the carryable, and the collectible. I don't think I'd care for Zern-y, Zerning, or Zerned—they lack scientific impact and precision. Use of the future tense is fine; if we just exercise common sense and don't drift into slang or puns, I think it will work out fine.

One last example: You couldn't read a Zern . . . but you could write one.

WHY I LIKE TO HUNT
WITH YOU

I've been thinking about why I especially like to hunt with you. I don't remember our ever having a day together that I didn't enjoy, because you care much more about why we are together in the field than about what we take away in game.

I like the fact that you don't talk too much, don't make excuses, and never brag—unless you say something nice about my dog, something more than being plain polite.

When we gun the covers that you've chosen, I know you always let me take the choicest spots and often pass up shots in hopes the bird will swing my way.

I know you count the few birds you've hit and lost against your limit, and I've seen you time and again refuse a chancy shot that might touch a bird we couldn't fairly bring to bag.

You always remember a little-something gift, and take some pleasant time to chat with the men that own the land we like to gun. You make a point of stopping in the local store to say hello.

You've always been on time, and do more than your share of the little things that make a hunt a happy day—regardless of the birds we've found, if any.

I always know that you know where I am in heavy cover. You are careful to let me know your whereabouts as well—and I have never, not once, looked down the end of your gun barrel. Nor do I ever expect to.

When the day is over and the guns are put away, you show me that your gun is empty. You know when to drink, how much, and when not to.

You never complain about being too hot or too cold or too tired—unless you think I might feel the need of leaving early, and somehow you make it easy then for me to say "Let's go." If you think I'm just plain tired, you say you are and suggest we sit and smoke a pipe and ease the dogs.

You always seem most pleased when I've had some sort of outstanding day. You never forget the few things I've done more or less well and tend to say "barely all right" about yourself, when in all fairness it was often just the other way around.

It seems you pick and clean more than your share of the birds—and then offer the most and the choicest to the rest of us.

You manage to keep the camp cheerful, claim you like to cook and wash and dry, as well as make sure of the wood supply.

And somehow, everywhere I go you're there. You turned up my Texas bunkie who helped me do my white-tail buck in half the time and twice as well as I'd have clumsied it through all alone.

I remember the time you gave me a stand that "wasn't very special," when we gunned an Arizona sunflower field for doves— and then you marked my birds and quit when I had gone the limit even though your gunning day was far, far less than you deserved.

We met in Pennsylvania gunning grouse, and somehow you put me just so behind your soft-footed little setter, where I got the kind of shots that even I can make.

You marked my singles down in waist-high South Carolina broom and never failed to say "Nice shot" when I took one bird where I think you might have taken two.

I remember how well you called the pintails in that Utah lake and how you let me take first shots at swinging honkers on the Eastern Shore.

Sometimes I've called you Tex, or Billy Joe or Little Jim or Pat. No matter now—like the outdoors gentleman you are—names don't mean a thing. I know we'll meet up again this fall, and I'll be all the richer for it.

You'll be the man who remembers to bring a flashlight, an extra sweater, and that I like my coffee black. And just in case I never said it to your face before, you're as big a reason as I know to spend a day outdoors. You make the days seem all too short and too few and far between, my treasured friend. You are everything that puts real meaning in that simple phrase: "a Sportsman."

ABOUT THE AUTHOR

GENE HILL is an associate editor of *Field & Stream,* writing a monthly column also under the title "Hill Country." He is a resident of New Jersey when he is not off fishing or shooting in Scotland, Mexico, Canada, or any state or country that offers an occasional bird or trout or bass. He is dominated by several Labrador retrievers, two daughters, his wife, and most of the membership of several shooting and fishing clubs. He admits to having more than two trap guns—ditto skeet guns and field guns. His fly-rod collection lacks both a Payne and a Garrison, which is why his children have been cutting back on their school lunches. A gifted stylist, his ability to turn a phrase is well exemplified by his description of himself as looking "like a badly tied fly." He is one of America's most widely read outdoor writers.